Sophie probably *was* Wednesday's child...

"For someone who has so many woes you certainly like to live dangerously, Lady Sophrina."

"Why are you calling me that?" Sophie asked, and Matthew shrugged.

"You really must forgive me. It's being a writer. I have this romantic imagination. I often see you as a lady of long ago—bright hair, flowing robes and glowing violet eyes."

Dear Reader,

Help us celebrate life, love and happy-ever-afters with our great new series.

Everybody loves a party, and birthday parties best of all, so join some of your favorite authors and celebrate in style with seven fantastic new romances. One for every day of the week, in fact, and each featuring a truly wonderful woman whose story fits the lines of the old rhyme, "Monday's child is..."

> *Monday's child is fair of face*
> *Tuesday's child is full of grace,*
> *Wednesday's child is full of woe,*
> *Thursday's child has far to go,*
> *Friday's child is loving and giving,*
> *Saturday's child works hard for its living,*
> *And a child that's born on a Sunday*
> *Is bonny and blithe and good and gay.*

(Anon.)

Does the day on which you're born affect your character? Some people think so—if you want to find out more, read our exciting new series. Available wherever Harlequin books are sold.

May	#3407	*The Marriage Business*	Jessica Steele
June	#3412	*Private Dancer*	Eva Rutland
July	#3417	*Coming Home*	Patricia Wilson
August	#3422	*Desperately Seeking Annie*	Patricia Knoll
September	#3424	*A Simple Texas Wedding*	Ruth Jean Dale
October	#3429	*Working Girl*	Jessica Hart
November	#3434	*Dream Wedding*	Helen Brooks

Happy reading,

The Editors, Harlequin Romance

Coming Home
Patricia Wilson

Harlequin Books

TORONTO • NEW YORK • LONDON
AMSTERDAM • PARIS • SYDNEY • HAMBURG
STOCKHOLM • ATHENS • TOKYO • MILAN
MADRID • WARSAW • BUDAPEST • AUCKLAND

ISBN 0-373-03417-2

COMING HOME

First North American Publication 1996.

Copyright © 1996 by Patricia Wilson.

Printed in U.S.A.

CHAPTER ONE

'I WISH you hadn't done it, Esther.' Sophie Grant looked up ruefully from the letter in her hand. 'I know it's just about boiled down to accepting this offer or sleeping in the park, but I'm not sure it was a good idea to pounce on what was probably just a polite enquiry. I don't know him, after all.'

'He wanted to know what had become of you,' Esther said firmly. 'You were ill so I took it upon myself to let him know. I was worried about you and getting that letter from your solicitor was a blessing.'

'Well, I suppose I'm lucky, really, having someone to go to...' Sophie's voice trailed away and Esther glanced at her keenly as she reached for her coat.

'I'm on duty in an hour, I'll have to go, but don't get any hang-ups about this,' she insisted. 'He offered to have you and that makes a lot of difference. He *is* your uncle.'

'He is not,' Sophie corrected. 'You know he isn't, Esther. Matthew Trevelyan is no relative at all. He was my father's stepbrother and I've only met him once, when I was thirteen. I thought he was a very worrying man. Not that he'll scare me now,' she added with a frown. 'I was probably impressionable then and he rather took me by surprise, being so dark-haired. Mummy called him Black Cornish.'

'Only because of his hair colour, surely? Nothing to do with his character,' Esther soothed briskly, and Sophie grinned up at her, her violet eyes over-large in a pale face.

5

'Unless she knew something I didn't,' she laughed. 'Mummy didn't like Matthew Trevelyan for some reason. She liked his wife even less.'

'Well, you don't have to make your mind up for a week. Finish your breakfast and then get a bit more sleep. We'll talk about it tonight and maybe come up with an alternative.'

Sophie nodded and smiled, but as Esther left her eyes turned again to the solicitor's letter and her mind went back to the problem. There was no alternative. In just under two weeks she would have nowhere to live, and unless she went to stay with her father's stepbrother sleeping in the park was a possibility that was not actually very remote.

It would have been bad enough if she had not been so ill but a particularly vicious attack of flu, followed by some unknown virus, had left her feeling weak and helpless, utterly unlike her normal, assertive self. She had just lost her job because the firm had gone into liquidation. Worse than that, the mean row of terrace houses where she had lived for almost three years with Esther Reed, an old schoolfriend, was to be demolished to make way for a new shopping arcade and car park. Esther was a nurse and was moving into the nurses' home until she got married, but Sophie had nowhere to go at all.

She had been in control of her life for so long now that she still felt stunned at the way things had fallen apart. She rested back on the pillows, determined to get the sleep that Esther insisted would restore her to health, but her mind began to relive the past, and she went back to a time four years ago when she had been told of her parents' death.

They had been archaeologists, working in Africa, and a sudden landslide at the dig had killed them both. It had been a shock but she had not suffered the overwhelming sadness that this sort of news would have brought to most daughters because she had never been close to them. All her life she had felt merely an encumbrance. Her time had been spent at boarding-school, and she had only seen them during the long holidays when they had come home, which they had always done, she felt, with reluctance. They hadn't even owned a house in England.

They had been academics first and last, and she could not remember any sort of love or warmth between them. They had admired each other, worked together and spoken intently about their latest work almost all the time. Sophie had always been left out and she had often wondered how she had come to be born.

Suddenly, at eighteen, she had been left completely alone and she had been called to London to hear about the provision that had been made for her. There was no money at all to get her started in life unless she fulfilled the terms of the short and coldly worded will.

The will had pointed out that she had always had the very best of schooling and that this had taken a great deal of money. The remaining money was solely for her education, providing that she pursued an academic career. They had suggested archaeology, anthropology or, as a concession, ancient history.

That was when Sophie had exploded with anger and dismay. Her future had been mapped out in the same cold manner in which her life so far had been planned. They had never wanted to know her own desires. She might just have been a well-behaved intruder for all the notice her parents had taken of her in her teenage years. Now, with no discussion about her future when they had been able to speak to her, they had laid down firmly that she would follow in their footsteps.

Sophie had raged, not even stopping when the solicitor had pointed out that if she refused there would be no support for her and nothing coming to her until she was thirty. She had made her opinion known in no uncertain terms and had gone back to school to pack her belongings and head for London and a new life.

She had been eighteen, healthy and clever; she'd been sure that getting a job would be no problem at all, and she would go to university when she felt like it. There had been a certain freedom in being able to decide for herself and the hurt had been buried as it had always been buried. She had resolved never to touch the money. She would get a grant when the time came.

That was the first time she had heard from Matthew Trevelyan. He had written from America when he had learned of the death of his stepbrother. He had wanted to know what she intended to do, but Sophie had instructed the solicitor to tell him that she was perfectly capable of managing her own affairs. She had no intention of stepping into the control of anyone—ever. Her life was her own and she would live it. Defiance was a burning emotion and she had been filled with rebellion against everyone who seemed to be in a position of authority.

Now, at twenty-two, she was different, ready to settle down. She had a place at university, and a grant had been allowed after much paperwork and insistence. But it was for September—six months from now—and in the meantime she was ill and would soon be homeless.

Out of the blue had come a further enquiry. After four years in America Matthew Trevelyan was now back in Cornwall and wanted to know what had become of her. His letter had been passed on while Sophie had been still too ill to cope. Esther had rung the solicitor, explaining the position, and now there was this offer of a refuge.

The idea made Sophie squirm. She was almost twenty-three, not a child to be looked after. She didn't know this man. He was just a shadow from the past—and he might be a worrying shadow but she had enough common sense to know that for now she could not manage alone. There seemed to be no way out of it.

She had not needed to tell Esther about Matthew because they had several of his books in the house. Sophie had bought them out of curiosity in the days when she had not been so short of cash. Seeing one on the best-seller shelf at the bookshop, she had bought it impulsively. After that she had bought more because they were fascinating.

She had to admit that the full-length photograph of the author on the back had not shown him exactly as she remembered him. Still, it had only been a brief meeting when she had gone with her father and mother to his wedding, and she had been no more than thirteen, her attitude definitely coloured by her mother's dislike of him.

Sophie got shakily from her bed and picked out one of the books now, sinking back into the pillows and turning the volume over to the back cover. There was the picture that she had looked at many times. It was a face she would in all probability be seeing very soon in real life. He looked uncompromising, and she bit into her lip a little anxiously as she studied him intently.

It was two years since she had bought the book. He probably looked worse by now. Esther had not read anything of his. She had been content simply to watch a film that had been made from one of his latest works and it had frightened her to bed. If she had read it instead she would have been even more frightened. It was impossible to get the nuances of the written word into a film.

The books were good, absorbing, but the choice of subject matter was weird and off-beat. He had the uncanny knack of picking out everyday things and situations and taking them to their worst conclusions. The writing was dark, alarming and just edged enough with the possibility of reality to chill the mind. The sex scenes were explicit too—that would have been more than enough for Esther.

Sophie's little grin at this thought died away as she looked at the image of the man himself. Black Cornish. She could see now what her mother had meant, although at thirteen she had been more impressed by the word 'black' than anything else. It had conjured up wickedness, cruelty and a certain amount of depravity—a picture that had made her stand very close to her mother and not even manage a smile when he had been introduced to her.

She wondered what he had made of her then. He had probably thought her dim-witted. More than likely, though, he hadn't thought anything at all. It had been his wedding-day and Sophie's memory was excellent; she had not forgotten the beautiful Delphine Trevelyan. She wondered what his wife looked like now, nine years later. How would she take to having a temporary guest?

Temporary she was certainly going to be because Sophie had no intention of staying in Cornwall any longer than was necessary. So far she had made quite a mess of her life, but this time she would set herself a steady path and stick to it.

She took one last look at the man she would soon be meeting—if she decided to take up his offer. She didn't need to read the words below the picture either. She knew that he had been a journalist on one of the big London papers. She also knew that he had given it up to write novels when he was only twenty-eight; she had read all that two years ago when she had bought the book. How old did it make him now—thirty-four? It must do, because her father had been twelve years older than his stepbrother.

The dark face looked steadily at her and she had a great desire to push the book back on to the shelf. It was a compelling face—lean, strong and intelligent. His hair was like jet and she remembered that. She remembered his eyes too—peculiar, amber. They had held the sharp glitter of ice at the wedding, and now she wondered why. If he could not show any joy on his wedding-day, what sort of man was he?

Worry flooded her mind but she pulled herself up sharply. She would only need to be with him for six months—from March to the beginning of September. By then, with a bit of luck, she would be secure and not in need of any help at all. She would be on her own again.

When Andrew Norton called round to see her two days later she told him, and he was filled with gloom and irritation.

'But Sophie, I'll not see you for ages!' he protested. 'It's a hell of a long way to Cornwall. You can't be going on the strength of a solicitor's letter!'

'Well, it's the only letter I'm likely to get,' she pointed out ruefully. 'I'm lucky he enquired. He must have a conscience, and I know he was very fond of my father. When I get settled in I'll probably be able to invite you for a weekend.'

She knew that she was speaking confidently to dispel her own worries. She needed reassurance but nobody could give her any. Matthew Trevelyan looked as forbidding to Esther and Andrew as he did to her. They had both studied the photograph rather glumly.

'Why don't you call him Uncle Matthew?' Andrew asked suspiciously.

'Because he's not my uncle. He's no relative at all.'

'Then it sounds like a dodgy situation to me. Don't go!' he said firmly. 'You won't know a soul and I don't like the look of him. I can't protect you from so far off.'

Sophie smiled. She was not normally in need of protection. She considered herself to be tough, in spite of her slender, long-legged appearance. But now she had no choice. She had already decided that. Most days she felt so low in energy that she had to stay in bed, and going to Cornwall had become almost a duty. She had no right to inflict herself on her friends. They were in no position to take care of her, and Matthew Trevelyan had offered.

She knew that Andrew was going to miss her, at least initially. They had been very good friends for almost a year and he had dropped all his other girlfriends to go out with her. Still, college was taking up a lot of his time; his finals were looming up, and he would not be pining alone in any case. He was good-looking enough to attract any girl.

'Let's get married!' he suggested eagerly and Sophie laughed at his lapse into drama.

'As a temporary solution to my problems?'

'We might like it enough to make it permanent,' he said more seriously, but Sophie kept up the smiles. Maybe it was a good idea to get away after all. Andrew was the sort of person who made quixotic offers but there was a look at the back of his eyes that worried her. He was given to bursts of jealousy too. She just didn't feel like that about him. He was a friend and that was how it had to stay.

One week later Sophie sat on the train that was taking her rapidly to the West Country, but she saw very little of the countryside that flashed by. She was in a state of self-recrimination. Had it not been for her burst of furious hurt and anger at life, coupled with her naturally defiant nature, she would not now be going to place herself at the mercy of a man she did not know.

Why hadn't she simply agreed to the terms laid down by her parents? She could easily have changed her course later. Like Andrew she would have been almost finished at university now instead of being in this mess.

She knew why, really. She had always known why: hurt—well-concealed hurt—and a feeling of being alone all her life. Now, as she viewed the changing landscape, she wished that she had looked for any alternative rather than this. The arrangements had been made unfeelingly through the solicitor. Matthew Trevelyan had offered her a temporary refuge but he had not written himself; he had just phoned the solicitor. She had little choice, though, because she needed a temporary refuge, needed to catch up on the studies she had neglected for four years, and she needed just a modicum of help.

All she had to do, according to Mr Brown of Wellington and Brown, was travel to Cornwall and things would take care of themselves. Well, here she was, on her way, and her natural defiance was not there at all. She still felt incredibly weak, and she had seen Esther's worried face as the train had pulled away. Sometimes the world seemed to spin around her and it was happening again as she stared out of the window of the speeding train.

She closed her eyes tightly and thought of meeting the man whose picture she had often looked at with curiosity. His offer seemed to be almost offhand. Perhaps there would be no refuge at all? He didn't know a thing about her; she was a stranger, and as the landscape became more remote, more alien, Sophie regretted this move. There was an uneasy tingling in her spine—a feeling of anxiety that was being compounded by her lingering feeling of weakness.

As the train pulled into the station she stood and began to gather her belongings. There were her suitcases and quite a few boxes that contained books and other possessions. It had been hilarious getting them on to the train, but then Esther and Andrew had been with her and they had been inclined to treat the whole thing as a joke.

They had both offered to come down with her but Sophie had refused. For one thing she was not used to being looked after, and for another they really could not afford either the time or the fare.

It was no joke now; in fact it was rather embarrassing. In the first place she had to get her belongings to the platform, and in the second she had no idea what Matthew Trevelyan would say when he realised that she had brought everything she possessed with her. There had been absolutely nowhere to leave it. She was left standing on the platform, surrounded by her clutter, when the train pulled out.

There was nobody to meet her and Sophie was filled with dismay. Even if Matthew Trevelyan had been detained, it seemed to show his offhand attitude very well. She was totally unimportant and could wait. What she would do if he failed to arrive at all she just did not know.

There were now only a few people on the platform and a cold wind was blowing that had the feel of the sea about it. She pulled her coat more closely around her, glad of its warmth, and her eyes met the interested scrutiny of a woman who was standing just inside the entrance. The locking of their glances seemed to break some sort of stupor as far as the woman was concerned, because she came across and spoke.

'This is probably foolish of me,' she confessed a trifle stiffly. 'I know it's most unlikely, but are you Sophrina Grant?'

It was Sophie's turn to stiffen. She was *never* called Sophrina. She hated it, and she looked back at the woman with none of the glad relief she should have been feeling.

'Yes,' she conceded, forcing a tight smile. 'I'm waiting to be collected. I'm going to Trembath House to stay with——'

'Oh, I know where you're going.' There was a rather forced smile on the woman's face too. 'Matt sent me to collect you, though what he'll make of you I'm sure I don't know.'

Her eyes ran with some exasperation over Sophie, noting the slender height, the long legs enclosed in bottle-green leggings, the matching short green coat trimmed with dark imitation fur. It emphasised the rich auburn glow of short curly hair, the chestnut lights glittering in the sun, and she didn't seem pleased with Sophie's appearance. Sophie was not amused either, to be inspected so minutely.

'He sent you to get me?' she enquired. 'You're his secretary?' She deliberately made her voice haughty, forcing her way back into her old attitude to life, and had the satisfaction of seeing the woman redden with annoyance. Two could play at most games and nobody was going to know that she dreaded meeting Matthew Trevelyan. It might have been a long time since she had seen his wife but this woman was not Delphine Trevelyan. Delphine had been a very pale blonde and the woman facing her was a brunette.

'Heavens, no! Working with Matt would be terrifying; he's not even civilised when he's working. We—er—we're friends.'

Friends! Yes, Sophie could imagine that. Her heart sank. Complications! She wondered what Delphine thought of this 'friend' of her husband.

'I'm doing this as a favour,' the woman continued. 'I'm Eve Corwin, by the way.' Belatedly she held out her hand and Sophie had no alternative but to accept it. It was withdrawn speedily and Eve turned her eyes to the piles of luggage at Sophie's feet.

'I see you don't travel lightly,' she muttered, with an irritated frown. 'Let's hope I can get it all into the car.'

'I'll be staying until September. I brought the things I would need.' She was not about to tell this woman that she had brought all her worldly goods. It was better to be thought extravagant than poor.

'September? Why, that's all of six months!' She gave Sophie one of her sweeps of inspection again and her lips tightened even further as she added, 'Goodness knows what Matt will think.'

'He invited me to stay,' Sophie assured her, with a growing irritation of her own. 'I'm sure he knows what to expect.' It was infuriating to be scanned for faults. As far as she knew she looked fine. These clothes were her very smartest and quite up to the minute as far as fashion was concerned. She had bought them before she'd known that she would be homeless and without a job.

'I don't think he quite knows what to expect,' Eve said coolly, bending reluctantly to help with the luggage. 'Matt asked me to fetch you because he's waiting for a very important call from America and couldn't come himself. He gave the impression that you were a teenager. You must have grown, Miss Grant,' she finished sarcastically.

'I grew a long time ago.' Sophie's mind catapulted into gloom when she realised why he had been willing to have her here. He must have been so involved with his books that he had failed to register the time since he had seen her last. 'He was my father's stepbrother. Actually, it's very good of him to ask me to stay.'

'His mind must have been on something else,' Eve murmured drily. 'Matt and "very good" do not sit easily in my imagination. Matt and "furious" rings more true. You'll have to watch your step, or I'll be bringing this lot back before long.' There was satisfaction in her voice and Sophie decided to keep quiet.

None of this was anything to do with this woman. As far as she could see, she would be less of a burden than some young girl, especially if he was the sort of absent-minded writer who forgot to put on his socks.

She glanced at the other woman as the car left the station and made her own assessment. The face was almost beautiful and immaculately made up. Even for this trip to the station she was wearing an expensive dark blue trouser suit. In all probability Eve never let her image slip at all, particularly in front of Matthew Trevelyan.

Sophie decided to be very cool with her. Under other circumstances she would have been grateful for the lift but Eve had antagonised her right from the first and she felt unable to relax now. There was little to see of the countryside at the moment because they were running along a narrow road between high grassy banks where the first spring flowers were showing.

The sun was beginning to shine, and when they topped a steep rise Sophie sat forward, unable to suppress a gasp of pleasure as the view opened before her. The road wound down to the sea and aimed itself at a small picturesque fishing village draped around the stone harbour walls. The sun was glinting on the water. It was high tide and a few boats rocked at anchor in the tranquillity of the harbour. The whole place would have been a delight for any artist to paint.

'Port Withian,' Eve said briefly, noticing her fascination. 'I live here.'

'You're very lucky,' Sophie mused aloud, and Eve made a snort of disgruntled agreement.

'In some ways. However, I'm more used to bright lights and interesting conversation. I'm not Cornish.'

'Neither am I,' Sophie confessed thoughtlessly, and got herself a suspicious stare.

'I thought you said that your father and Matt...?'

'My father was not Cornish, neither was my mother, and as I was born in Sussex I can't see any way I could lay claim to being Cornish, can you?'

Once again Sophie was wishing that she had remained silent. One slip and Eve pounced. She was suspicious and antagonistic for no good reason as far as Sophie could tell, and Sophie hoped that she would be seeing very little of her, even though she was a friend of Matthew.

The car sped down the hill and entered the village. Sophie's nerves tightened up as she began to look around for some sign of a dwelling that could be called Trembath House. There were just picturesque cottages, though, nothing big enough to contain an author of international acclaim, although his address had been Port Withian.

They sped through the village, skirting the harbour wall, and within minutes they were climbing again, until Sophie could look out at miles of sea. Away from the shelter of the harbour it was not so tranquil and, even on this sunny day, the waves crashed spectacularly on the rocks far below. It looked wild and dangerous and the thought of how it would look in a storm almost made her shudder.

With the fishing village left behind there was an untamed look about the land, a feeling again of being in an alien landscape. There was a stormy restlessness about the sea and sky and she was suddenly reminded of the way Matthew's eyes had looked so many years ago, reflecting the turbulence of a clever mind, irritated by circumstances. It made Sophie uneasy and she clasped her hands together, wishing herself miles away.

The journey had shaken her more than she had expected. She felt dizzy again, worn out, and all she wanted was a hot drink and a chance to sleep. It seemed like madness to have come all this way but even now she could not think of another thing she could have done. It was going to be terrible to face a stranger and confess to feeling ill. She tightened her lips and acknowledged that she would not be confessing anything of the sort. Somehow she would manage. She always did.

As they came to the top of the hill she could see a house on the headland. It stood proudly facing the sea; there was a sort of inevitability about it that spoke of age and strength and the fortitude to face the challenge of waves and wind. It was backed by trees, and green lawns stretched around it, dotted here and there with bushes that softened the picture of a house defying the elements.

Something inside her stirred at the sight of it—fear and excitement—and she found herself wishing almost frantically that they would just drive past, that this was not where Matthew Trevelyan lived. Inside, though, she knew it was and it was no surprise when Eve murmured in a satisfied voice, 'Here we are. This is Trembath House.'

Sophie just stared at it, noting its size and the almost unforgiving look about the grey stone of its walls, the long windows that faced the sea and the wide drive that led to the house itself. There were huge banks of rhododendrons, not yet in bloom. Whatever else struggled with the elements, these did not. They flanked the drive and lent strength to the trees behind the house, their foliage already adding a sombre beauty to the place.

'Do you know what Trembath means?' Eve murmured, noting Sophie's expression. 'It means place of the grave. Forbidding, isn't it?'

'It's quite exciting,' Sophie countered, not about to show her inner anxieties in front of a stranger. 'There's something wild about it, quite in keeping with the sea and sky. I can understand why a writer would want to live here.'

'Well, I can tell you why Matt lives here,' Eve snapped, no doubt disappointed that her earlier words had not alarmed Sophie into instant flight. 'It's where he was born. He should be in London. I sometimes think he lives here out of sheer spite!'

Sophie glanced at her sharply, but the beautiful mouth was tightly closed, the well-made-up face stiff with annoyance. There would be no further enlightenment and she was greatly relieved. She had not wanted to know that this was the place of the grave, and she had not wanted to know that anyone could live somewhere out of sheer spite.

Her hands clenched more tightly together and she did a very rapid mental calculation of how much it would cost to go straight back to London and forget the whole thing. Six months in a park did not now seem so alarming.

Deep down she knew, and had always known, that Matthew Trevelyan did not want her here. He had cared about her father but she had a lingering impression from her youth that he cared about little else. He had even seemed annoyed with his own wedding.

Nobody greeted them as the car stopped in front of the house, and Eve instantly began to unload Sophie's luggage as if she wanted the things out of her car and out of her sight as speedily as possible. Almost before Sophie could help they were dumped unceremoniously on the gravel of the drive in front of the short flight of steps that led to the door.

'No great welcoming committee,' Eve stated with satisfaction, glancing at Sophie's strained face. 'Don't be surprised. Matt doesn't care much for people.' She led the way into Trembath House, opening the door without ringing the bell, and showing Sophie into a wide hall that was also deserted.

A flight of stairs led to the upper rooms, curving out of sight, the banisters white-painted and elegant. The house was more welcoming than it had looked from outside and the high gloss of the hall floor caught the rather fitful rays of the sun. Doors opened off the hall to the downstairs rooms, and if she had been alone Sophie would have simply stood and waited, because, she admitted to herself, she was by now rather intimidated.

She wanted to sit down with an almost desperate longing, but she felt compelled to help as Eve left her and marched off down the steps, to bring in the suitcases with an air of martyrdom. As one of the doors opened Sophie knew exactly why the other woman was putting on such a show—Matthew was at home and Eve was determined that he should see just how useless and dependent his visitor was going to be.

Sophie was turning to fetch more luggage as the door opened, but she stopped at the sight of the man who stepped into the hall, her breath catching in her throat. He hadn't changed at all. He was exactly like the photograph, exactly as Sophie remembered him from so long ago, but not *quite* the same. She was seeing him now through grown-up eyes and she stiffened with alarm.

He was tall enough to be intimidating—broad-shouldered, lean-hipped, with an odd, animal grace about him that she had not noticed in her childish anxiety at his wedding. The face was the same, though—dark, clever, striking—but it was almost overshadowed by those eyes.

They were peculiar, cat-like eyes, with the amber beauty of some dangerous hunting creature—eyes that were very much alive. They flared over her and then narrowed as he stared at her, his brow beginning to furrow in a questioning way.

'Sophrina?' Matthew Trevelyan's dark eyebrows rose in obvious astonishment, his tawny eyes searching her rather tight expression.

'Sophie,' she corrected firmly. 'Nobody calls me Sophrina.'

It was better to start as she meant to go on. Her soft lips were rather compressed. She had no idea what to call him. He was not her uncle, and as she contemplated that she thought uneasily of Andrew's concern. She was not with a relative. Who *was* she with? It now seemed to be a great liberty to have come here. His offhand enquiry had probably been made when some memory of her father had surfaced. He had possibly expected no reply at all, and now she felt as if she had swooped on him like a vulture.

It was alarming too to realise that he was having an odd effect on her. She had gone on thinking about him as a child would think, remembering the impression he had left with her. Mentally she had placed him in her father's age-group but he was not like that. He was a virile, disturbing man who had nothing to do with her at all.

Looking at a photograph had in no way prepared her. He was giving off an aura of tightly controlled power that seemed to be a mixture of strength and intelligence and something almost sexual. She could quite see why Eve wanted to linger and Sophie frantically wanted a sight of his wife; a woman with the authority to settle things down would be welcome at this moment.

'Forgive me,' he said drily. 'Time seems to have passed me by. Your father called you Sophrina.'

'Not when I was old enough to have a say in the matter,' she stated with shaky inflexibility.

'Well, you're certainly old enough to decide your own fate now,' he muttered, his tawny gaze running over her slowly. 'The family looks,' he murmured. 'Auburn hair and violet eyes. They didn't look quite so striking on Quentin.'

'Didn't you realise that little girls grow up?' Eve asked waspishly.

'Apparently not.' He gave Sophie another searching glance. 'However, I'm now recovered from the shock. I'll get your things taken up to your room.' He strode across the hall and opened a door before shouting at the top of his voice, 'Biddy!'

The phone began to ring as a small, plump middle-aged woman appeared, wiping her hands on her apron, and Matthew nodded vaguely towards Sophie.

'See to her, will you, Biddy?' he asked shortly. 'That's my call. I'll get her things in a minute.'

He disappeared into the room that seemed to be his study, ignoring them all, and after one exasperated look at the closed door Eve Corwin turned to go, her final glance at Sophie filled with boiling irritation.

CHAPTER TWO

SOPHIE was not irritated. She was almost afraid, but she was here, firmly entrenched, and as she was here for just a short time she would cope with anything. Besides, Matthew Trevelyan would forget that she was in his house very quickly. He would look at her vaguely and put her out of his mind. It suited her fine and she turned to the rosy-cheeked woman who stood smiling at her.

'I'm Sophie Grant,' she said quietly. It was a relief to see this wholesome woman and Sophie stood on trembling legs as Biddy shook her hand.

'I'm pleased to meet you, Miss Grant. I've got your room ready, although I was told that you were, well, very young...'

'It's just a mix-up,' Sophie informed her with a smile. 'I think Mr Trevelyan forgot me. Don't call me Miss Grant, please. Just Sophie.'

'Well, I don't know what Mr Trevelyan will say,' Biddy mused, and Sophie began to get her scattered things together, her cheeks flushed with exertion.

'He'll never notice, I'm sure,' she muttered.

He wouldn't either. She would have plenty of time to study here because she would be in complete silence, unless Biddy was the type to hang around and talk. All the same, it was a little worrying. He had quite clearly offered to have her because he had thought that she was still too young to be on her own. His attitude when he had seen her was indicative of that. He had looked stunned and slightly irritated.

It would have been interesting to know why he had gone on ignoring her existence for four years. If he had expected a teenager now, what could he have expected then? Still, he had been in America so perhaps he had just left well alone. Fortunately, things had gone smoothly until recently and she had been more than capable of looking after herself.

Sophie sighed as she climbed the stairs, following Biddy, both of them weighed down by luggage, with plenty more to bring up. It was no business of hers what Matthew Trevelyan thought. It was a refuge here—a short-term refuge. She would keep out of his way and be very polite when they met. Being anything else would be a bit dangerous, she admitted to herself. He looked much more worrying now than he had done when she'd been a child. How she would cope with his wife was another matter. Matthew might have worried her but she had memories of her mother's downright dislike when she thought of Delphine Trevelyan.

'Here we are, then!' Biddy's cheerful remark brought Sophie out of her speculations and she walked into a bedroom that stood at the beginning of a passage at the top of the stairs.

It was a beautiful room—big, with a window that looked out over the garden and across to the sea. It was bright and airy and she could not help comparing it with the small, dark room that she had occupied for the past four years.

'There's your bathroom through there,' Biddy pointed out, nodding at a door at the side of the room. 'Not all the rooms have bathrooms attached but this one does, and Mr Trevelyan's too. I hope this is all right?'

'Of course! It's a lovely room and I can see the sea from the window.'

'This has always been a beautiful house, even when I was a young maid here,' Biddy murmured, her eyes going round the room. 'It hasn't been a happy house, though.' Sophie looked at her in surprise and she flushed guiltily. 'Listen to me gossiping,' she said in a scandalised voice. 'And I can tell you that Mr Trevelyan is as good as they come—always has been. I'll get the rest of your things.'

She hurried out and Sophie followed her slowly. There was still a lot of luggage to get up here and she had to help, but she really felt weak now. Many more trips up the stairs and she was going to fall down them. She was very quiet, and puzzled too. Why had Biddy said that this was not a happy house? Obviously Biddy had known Matthew for a long time—probably all his life if she had been a maid here. Why did he stay here if it was not a happy place?

She remembered Eve's assertion that Matthew lived here out of sheer spite. What had that meant? A dark, intriguing man in an intriguing house. A man of mystery. Maybe he had to sit in this house and collect the atmosphere for his books. How did his wife take to it, and how did she take to Eve Corwin?

It was all a bit gothic, Sophie concluded as she went back up the stairs with another load of things. She was really shaking, and lagged far behind Biddy.

'All right, are you?'

She straightened up, nodding firmly at the anxious enquiry. So far nobody knew that she was still feeling ill. She didn't intend that they should find out either. Just a few minutes' sit-down and she would be all right, but she just could not make any more trips down the stairs.

'You settle here for a minute,' Biddy insisted, looking at her more closely. 'It's a long journey from London. I expect you're tired. I'll make a tray of tea for you and bring it up. You can drink it as you sort your things out. With a few biscuits it will put you on until dinnertime.'

'If it's no bother...' Sophie began, and Biddy's face creased into smiles.

'Bless you, no, miss! I'm looking forward to having you around here. You'll maybe brighten the place up.'

'Call me Sophie. Do you live in?' she added as the thought struck her.

'No, I live in Port Withian. I'm here every day, though, at seven, and I go after the dinner things are cleared.'

She went out to make the tea and Sophie sat on the edge of the bed. The room was swimming and she closed her eyes. This was not too good. She should have met Delphine before she'd settled in here. Maybe she was out. Again it spoke of indifference but Sophie was quite used to that. She was here. She had made it all in one piece. She would take things as they came.

She was just contemplating the walls of the room, which now seemed to have stopped spinning round, when there was a sharp tap on the door and her host stuck his head in. She instantly went on to danger alert, standing and facing him. Dark power seemed to come with him, washing around her, and he looked at her unwaveringly as he walked into the room.

'I said that I would get these up here for you,' he said sharply as his eyes fell on her heap of possessions. 'Don't attempt to fetch the rest up.'

'Biddy helped.' Sophie managed a slight smile. 'I'm going to put everything away now...' Her voice trailed off as he simply stood and watched her. There was no telling at all what he was thinking. He was as dark as he had ever been. Black Cornish. Only those incredible eyes seemed to have life and meaning and they were almost burning her. 'I'm not going to be any sort of nuisance,' she blurted out, more loudly than she had expected, and she saw his lips quirk as one black brow shot upwards in surprise.

'That's a relief. Have you just made this decision or has it always been your intention?'

She felt her face flushing hotly at the wry words but she fixed him with unflinching eyes.

'I was just pointing out that I don't intend to—to get under your feet or to presume upon your kindness in having me here. I don't intend to overstay my welcome.'

'Such as it is,' he finished for her, taking the words right out of her head. He put his hands in his pockets and leaned against the door, the tawny eyes now flashing with amusement. 'You grew up, Sophie. I'm not quite used to it yet. Somehow I had this distorted picture of you in my mind—a little girl. Of course, I realised that you would have grown, but instead of working it out mathematically I simply substituted another picture.'

'I—I expect writers do that,' she offered shakily, wishing that he would take his eyes from her face and look at the great muddle her things had made of the room. 'Er—I hope I can find somewhere to put all this stuff,' she ventured, and that did the trick. He stopped staring at her and glanced at her possessions.

'Just say what you want and I can practically guarantee that we have it somewhere in the house. Sort it out and let me know.'

'A bookcase?' she prompted.

'As soon as I have the rest of your things up here.' He looked at her closely. 'Are you still not well?'

'I—I'm just tired. Biddy is making me some tea but I really ought to meet your wife first.'

The searching look he had been giving her faded instantly as she spoke. He seemed to freeze over right in front of her eyes, and the way his lips tightened to one straight line was enough to tell her that she had said something terrible.

'My wife died seven years ago,' he said stiffly. He turned to leave at once and she moved forward impulsively, her hand outstretched.

'I'm so sorry. I didn't know. I would never have said...'

Her voice was so obviously distressed that he turned back, looking at her coolly.

'Don't let it worry you. She died in an accident while you were still a girl. How could you have known?'

'I'm sorry,' Sophie said desperately. 'I—I've made you remember and I never meant...'

'Sophie!' Even the sharp sound of his voice didn't help. The room spun faster, the deep blue of the carpet rose towards her, and she fainted in slow motion long before he could reach her.

When she came round she was on the bed and Matthew was at the door, roaring for Biddy. Sophie was too dazed to make out if his voice was worried or angry, and before she could reach any conclusions he had come back to her.

'Lie still!' he ordered as she made a move to sit up. 'When Biddy comes up she can get you into bed.' He was taking off her shoes and she desperately wanted to get up and be normal.

'I'll be all right,' she insisted. 'I—I expect I was tired.'

'Stop pretending, Sophie!' The glittering amber eyes shot a look at her before they went back to his task. 'The solicitor told me you had been ill and obviously you still are. It's lucky you made it here without fainting on the way.'

She was dismayed at the anger in his voice, her feeling of being a burden quite overwhelming her, and she looked across with relief as Biddy hurried into the room.

'Help her to get undressed and into bed,' he ordered. 'I'll go down and phone the doctor.'

'I don't really need . . .' Sophie began, but all she got was a piercing look as he left the room. He didn't even bother to answer.

'There now. I thought you looked pale and ill,' Biddy murmured anxiously. 'I should never have let you help with those heavy cases.'

'I only fainted,' Sophie managed in a placating voice, but Biddy pursed her lips and started undressing her like a well-trained nurse.

'I should have seen,' she stated uncompromisingly. 'There was I, chattering away, and you ready to drop. What the doctor will say I just don't know.'

'Don't tell him,' Sophie suggested weakly. 'I can manage,' she added as the firm, plump hands came to her blouse.

'Mr Matthew said to help.'

Sophie just left her to it. Everything was hazy anyway. It was interesting too that, under pressure, Biddy said Mr Matthew and not Mr Trevelyan. It more or less proved that she had known him as a boy.

She pulled herself up sharply. Here she was, letting her mind wander when she should have been thinking about her present predicament. This was awful! Now she was more than ever at the mercy of a man she didn't know at all. He must think her a great nuisance. He was probably regretting his charitable gesture in having her here. She had been determined not to be a burden, but what was she now? He would think that she had come here simply to lounge about and be looked after.

The arrival of the doctor stopped any further musing, and she had to tell him the whole story about her attack of flu and the virus.

'Travelling this far won't have helped,' he murmured sympathetically. 'Stay in bed for the rest of the day and then take it very slowly. Only time will sort this out. Just be sure you don't get chilled or overtired.'

Sophie stared glumly at the door as he left and then made a decision. She simply could not stay in bed and be looked after. Who was there to look after her except Biddy? It seemed that Biddy already had enough to do and, in any case, she went home after the evening meal.

She reached for her dressing-gown and was halfway into it when the door opened and Matthew stood there, contemplating her coolly.

'Er—I'm just getting up again,' she explained, aware of her state of undress. Being in a dressing-gown in front of a strange man would have been bad enough but she hadn't even managed to get into it yet.

'I distinctly remember that you promised not to be a nuisance.' He walked forward purposefully and she had trouble standing her ground.

'I meant it too. That's why I'm getting up.' She looked at him as firmly as possible but he ignored her completely.

'You'll be less of a nuisance in bed than you would be fainting all over the house,' he murmured. His hands were deftly removing her dressing-gown and she was stunned as he swung her up into his arms. 'Back into your nest, Sophie. The doctor told me exactly what you had to do and there is no way at all of escaping his orders. The rest of the day in bed and then you take things slowly until you're better.'

'I was well enough to travel and it's only because I was tired . . .' Her voice sounded shaky even to her own ears. She was shocked to find that his arms were warm, strong and safe. So far she had known very few members of the opposite sex and they had all been her own age, well aware of their growing manhood, rather self-obsessed. Matthew Trevelyan wasn't like that at all. He was well used to his manhood and clearly never thought of it. He made her feel small and quite insignificant.

'Arguing will get you nowhere at all,' he muttered, tucking her into bed, 'and if Biddy and I have to search the house to find you—there'll be trouble.' He straightened up and looked down at her seriously. 'Stop worrying about being a burden. I invited you here.' His lips twisted in amusement. 'The fact that you arrived somewhat battered is neither here nor there.'

'I never intended——'

'To be a nuisance. I know. We've established that.' He turned to the door and then glanced at the heap of things on the floor. 'I'll get the rest of your things up here and then sort them out for you.'

'No!' Sophie's rather sharp denial had him spinning round to look at her again. 'I—I mean they're all muddled up and—and I'll have to sort them myself. In any case,' she added rather desperately as he continued to stare at her with those strange, cat-like eyes, 'they're— they're private.'

'How intriguing. A spy in our midst. What an odd child you are, after all, Sophrina.'

He walked out and she stared after him, biting furiously at her lip, not knowing whether to be annoyed or embarrassed. She was not a child in any way at all and he damned well knew it! All the same, she had made herself look extremely foolish just because she didn't want him wasting his expensive time sorting out her books and things.

The fact that he had called her Sophrina had been deliberate too. But when she looked at the situation coolly the annoyance won over the embarrassment and her face set into stubborn lines as she heard him coming back up with the rest of her stuff.

A few minutes later he straightened up after arranging things neatly by the wall.

'We don't want you falling over them in the night, do we?' he murmured. He turned to look at her and she could see a sort of devilish light in his eyes that promised trouble. Sophie got her word in first.

'Please don't call me Sophrina.' It was a mixture of an order and a plea. It was meant to be aloof, commanding, but at the last second her nerve deserted her and he obviously knew that.

'I promise,' he assured her, 'providing that you stop behaving like a poor, unwanted little waif. Your father lived in this house. His daughter is very welcome here.'

'But I don't know you and it seems such a cheek. I— I mean we're not any sort of relatives. I'm not your niece.'

'No. We do have a sort of relationship, though. Your father meant a lot to me—more than you could imagine. I would look after you for his sake, even if you were not such a fascinating subject.' His lips tilted in a smile of pure mockery. 'An indisposed guest with very private possessions. What writer could resist the challenge?' His eyes skimmed over her fiery hair and deep violet eyes, lingering on her flushed cheeks, her pallor gone under his taunting gaze. 'Glowing Technicolor too, very easy to describe.'

She glared at the closed door as he left. She might be in glowing Technicolor—who wouldn't be after an encounter with him?—but she wasn't Black Cornish with eyes like a tormenting cat. She settled down huffily against the pillows and decided that she was in the safest place after all. If she had not fainted she would have had to eat dinner facing Matthew Trevelyan, and at the moment she was not at all up to that task.

As things turned out, Sophie was in bed for two days, and during that time she saw absolutely nothing of Matthew. Biddy looked after her very cheerfully and left things for her before the day ended. Matthew never even popped his head round the door to say goodnight, and it seemed to Sophie that this was indicative of how he would treat her for the duration of her stay. She was to be ignored.

Once, when she had had a quick shower, she came back into the bedroom to find that he had brought a bookcase up. He never came back to ask if it was all right. She was left with the impression that he had looked in, found to his relief that she was not there and had taken the opportunity to nip in and leave the bookcase. Well, if he intended to ignore her, she would assist him.

On the third day she was up bright and early. She felt well now. Plenty of rest and Biddy's good cooking had done the trick, and Sophie was just going down the stairs when the door opened and Matthew came into the hall. He was in jeans and a black sweater, a damp towel flung over his shoulder, and it was obvious that he had been for a swim.

Sophie just stared at him in astonishment. It was still cold and she had been watching the rather wild sea from her window before she'd come down.

'Good morning, Sophie.' His lips quirked at her expression and he dropped the towel on to a chair in the hall. 'Feeling better?'

'Yes, thank you.' She went on staring at him and then blurted out, 'You've been swimming!' She could hear the sound of accusation in her voice and he glanced at her with raised brows.

'I normally swim before breakfast. Old habits die hard. Your father and I used to be racing down the cliff path as soon as the sun was up. However,' he added seriously, 'don't let me catch you trying it. I know the tides and the currents. It's dangerous along this coast.'

'When it's warm I'll paddle,' she muttered, still watching his gleaming black hair, quite stunned that she considered him to be attractive, in a scary sort of way.

'Let's eat!' He walked off towards the breakfast-room and Sophie followed, picking up the damp towel *en route* in an absent-minded manner. He had an imperious disregard for things, she mused, noticing the way the towel had left a dull mark on the gleaming old wood of the chair.

'Just what do you intend to do with that?' Matthew had stopped to open the door for her, and when she looked up he was eyeing the towel sternly.

'It's wet. It will spoil the wood, and by the look of it that chair in the hall is an antique and——'

'Don't make the mistake of trying to reorganise my ways, Sophie Grant!' Before she could move, a hard hand had grasped her chin, tilting her face to the light. 'If I want to toss down a wet towel, I will toss it wherever I wish. Biddy has been collecting that wet towel for years. You'll probably find that I have a lot of nasty habits. Ignore them. I'm attached to them all.'

Her violet eyes flashed sparks but she knew that she had no right to shout at him even if she felt like it.

'I'm really sorry. It was an automatic action. Women do that sort of thing. In future I'll be very careful not to offend you.'

He could hear the tone of her voice and his eyes narrowed as he stared into the furious purple of hers. For a second the hand tightened on her face and then he let her go, suavely motioning her into the room ahead of him, taking the towel from her grasp as she passed him.

'Your ''automatic action'' will probably give Biddy a nasty turn,' he murmured sarcastically. 'With no towel in the hall she'll imagine that I've drowned.'

'I'll put it back!' Sophie turned on him only to find him grinning down at her, his peculiar eyes dancing with malicious amusement.

'A bad temper,' he noted. 'I can't think where you got that from. Quentin was a very even-tempered man and your mother was cool as a cucumber.'

She wanted to point out that she had been given every opportunity to develop her own character as she had mostly been alone. She would also have liked to mention that even if her mother had been cool she had been sufficiently heated to dislike him. As it was, she thought it best to be silent, especially as Biddy appeared and put a tray of tea on the table, walking off with the offending towel with no comment at all.

Matthew didn't say anything either and she supposed that she should have been grateful for that. He had treated her like a child but he had not brought Biddy into things. All the same, Sophie felt like walking out of the room. She couldn't, though. In the first place she was a guest here and had to do more or less as she was told. In the second place she was hungry, and as Biddy came in with hot plates carrying a hearty breakfast of bacon, eggs, sausages and kidney she eyed the food gleefully.

'What do you intend to do today, Sophie?'

There it was again, that taunting, patronising tone, and she looked up from her meal with cool eyes.

'I have to organise my things first. Then I expect I'd better get started on my work. I have a lot to do before term starts in September.'

'Take it easy at first. Don't forget you've been ill.' He looked quite serious and she nodded. She didn't want to be confined to bed again. 'What are you going to call me?' He was still looking at her as he asked this startling question and she went a little pink. It had been bothering her too. So far she had managed not to call him anything at all, and what she would have liked to call him when he was taunting and patronising was not at all suitable.

'You're not my uncle!' she stated firmly, wanting that right out of the way.

'Agreed,' he nodded. 'We've covered that ground already. Calling me "you" for a good length of time will be tricky, though, don't you think? How about using my name? Most people manage it without much trouble.'

Sophie gulped uneasily. Stupid it might have been but she had the decided feeling that when she started to call him by his name she would be putting herself at a disadvantage. He was right, though; she had given some thought to addressing him as 'you'.

Eve Corwin's familiarity came into her mind and she felt her face stiffen. She was not about to call him Matt.

'Matthew,' she said quietly, glancing up quickly when he made no comment. He was watching her with a strange smile on his face.

'Nobody ever calls me that,' he admitted softly, and she supposed that it was a bit formal. Besides, she had laid down the law about not being called Sophrina.

'I could call you Matt...' It was a reluctant gesture and he knew it.

'Please don't. I like the way you say Matthew in that odd, husky voice of yours. Let's leave it at that, shall we?'

She nodded and got back to her breakfast, very pleased when Biddy came in and began to bustle about with plates and toast. He had made a big deal about his name but, in all fairness, she had made a big deal about hers too. She pondered his remarks. Nobody had mentioned her 'odd, husky voice' before. When she got back to her room she would try it out.

'I've been thinking about you while you were ill in bed,' he suddenly said, apropos of absolutely nothing, and she felt a flustering attack of nerves coming on again.

'Er—yes?' she managed, in a flat little voice. She supposed that he had been thinking about her. He had probably been muttering to himself that she was all manner of a pest.

'I know you were in need of help, but how did it come about that you were in need of such rapid help? Your friend Esther described the situation as desperate, apparently. What was the desperation?'

Sophie bit her lip and glanced upwards at him; he was looking extremely calm and quite good-natured but she didn't exactly want to trot out all her problems. She had felt that he would know. There seemed to be no way out of it, though.

'It all began when they decided to pull the house down,' she said earnestly, and Matthew gave her his undivided attention. He even put his knife and fork down to watch her more closely, and she had the feeling that his mouth was slightly twitching although as far as she could see there was nothing amusing about her story. He didn't laugh, however, and she continued warily, 'They decided to build a car park where the street was and that was that.'

'Unfortunate,' he murmured. 'Didn't the authorities offer to rehouse you and your friend?'

'No. You see, the houses were sort of condemned when Esther and I moved in.' That wiped any faint amusement from his face and Sophie knew that it sounded bad, but they *had* made the place very nice, really, once the door was locked and the lights were on—if you didn't mind a lot of damp.

'So you were about to become homeless?'

'I wouldn't have minded that but I also lost my job. I was made redundant.' She rushed on as his eyebrows shot up, 'I couldn't have afforded a place of my own and Esther was moving into the nurses' home until she got married. She's getting married in the summer.' He just went on staring at her in an astounded sort of way and she gabbled out the rest of the sorry story. 'Then I got the flu and—and a virus.'

It sounded pretty grim and Matthew sat back and let his eyes roam over her face. She could really have done very well without those odd eyes watching her, especially as the amusement was back with a vengeance.

'"Wednesday's child is full of woe,"' he quoted silkily. 'Do you think this run of misfortune is about to continue?'

'I was doing all right until then,' she muttered, feeling the colour race into her cheeks. She could understand his anxiety about her misfortunes. He probably thought that she was under some peculiar black spell that would transmit itself to him. 'I've never had bad luck before,' she asserted a little more firmly.

'I suppose it all depends on what you call bad luck,' Matthew murmured softly. 'You haven't exactly been surrounded by a loving family.'

'What you've never had you never miss,' she said firmly, if untruthfully. 'I was all right. In any case, I can take care of myself normally.'

'I'm sure you can,' he agreed quietly. 'However, for the time being you don't have to. You're quite safe here.'

'Th-thank you.' Sophie gave him a quick glance again but he was not looking at her. He was gazing out of the window towards the sea, an odd expression on his face, and once again she was struck by his dark and fascinating looks. The sunlight was catching the blue-black lights in his hair and turning his eyes to the amber of some predatory animal. He should have been frightening but somehow he was not, even though he was definitely Black Cornish, as black as some rakish pirate from long ago.

Back in her room she found that she was just wasting her time. The sight of the sea fascinated her. It was wild, free—something she had never been able to be herself.

There was something stormy and wild about the house, too, and in spite of Matthew's power she realised that she felt at home here. Maybe it was a desire for roots. Her father had lived in this house, her grandmother too, and it was really the first time that she had been able to discover a past.

She had a great urge to see the grounds, to stand on the cliff-top and view the sea at closer quarters, and it was not long before she abandoned her room and made for the hall and the great outdoors.

Matthew was nowhere to be seen, but she could hear work-like noises coming from his study and she escaped thankfully through the front door before he could come out and spot her. It was sunny, and even though there was a stiff wind blowing from the sea it was pleasant and invigorating.

Sophie set off into the gardens, which stretched to the top of the cliff. They were well tended and would be very colourful in summer. The high hedges sheltered the lawn from the worst of the wind and, turning to look back at the house, she could only feel pleasure. What a contrast to her little terrace house and the mean streets that surrounded it.

The sea drew her like a magnet and soon she was standing on the top of the cliff, the wind blowing her short, bright curls as she looked out at the vast stretch of sea, cold and grey in this weather, the white tips of the waves catching the fitful sunlight. It was easy to understand why Matthew had told her not to attempt to swim. There was a rage about the water, and even from here she could hear the seething pull of the undertow.

She leaned forward to get a better view of the beach and gave a little shriek of alarm as a hand grasped her arm and pulled her back.

'What the devil are you doing?' Matthew was furious and Sophie turned to look up into his tight, dark face.

'I'm looking around.' She couldn't understand his anger but her quiet words did nothing to placate him.

'You're on the very edge of the cliff. If I have to follow you around, keeping you out of danger, I'll get nothing done at all.'

'I didn't ask you to follow me around,' she managed unevenly. He sounded cruel, resentful, and her feeling of roots vanished immediately. She was back to being a stranger and a nuisance, and that was nothing new.

'I'm supposed to wait until you fall over the cliff?' he snarled, and she pulled free and turned to the house, her bubbling spirit quite crushed. It was not easy to consider a battle with a man like Matthew Trevelyan.

'Perhaps it would be better if I went back to London,' she muttered. 'I wouldn't like to be the one to stop your writing, to interrupt your busy and important life——'

'Don't be so damned stubborn,' he bit out. 'You wouldn't be here if you had anywhere else to go!'

'I've got friends,' she snapped. She swung towards him angrily, betraying the tears that stood in her eyes, and his expression softened from rage to rueful compassion.

'Oh, Sophie. I can see that I'll have to mend my ways with you around.' He took her arm again, leading her away from the cliff and into the garden. 'Come on. It's warmer here, sheltered from the wind.'

His voice had softened too and she had to agree that it was decidedly warmer in the garden. The sun was not at all strong but the bushes and trees made the wide expanse of lawn into a suntrap that instantly warmed her chilled skin. She was wearing jeans and a thick sweater but obviously she would need a jacket if she went near the sea, not that she would be going there. Matthew was going to make life uncomfortable. He was going to spy on her too.

'I'm not trying to make you feel unwelcome, Sophie,' he murmured, as if he was picking up her thoughts. 'Seeing you there gave me a nasty jolt, though, especially with that bright hair. You looked so much like your grandmother—Quentin's mother.' He was silent for a second and then he added quietly, 'She fell from the cliff almost at that spot. I had this damnable feeling that I wouldn't be able to get to you in time.'

Sophie turned to him, her wide eyes searching his face.

'She died? Daddy's mother fell and died there?'

'Yes.' Matthew looked grim and turned her back to the house, his jaw tight. 'Your grandmother meant a lot to me. She was the only bright thing in this whole bloody house. Don't go there again, Sophie!'

CHAPTER THREE

MATTHEW let Sophie go and walked back to the house, stalking off like an angry animal, leaving her in the garden. But now she had no desire to wander about and explore. His amber eyes had looked empty for a moment. It was easy to imagine that nobody had problems like your own, she mused, but Matthew's stepmother had died years ago and if it still hurt then why did he stay here? He was rich; he had wealth beyond her unsophisticated imaginings. If the house and the memories upset him then why didn't he just go?

Eve's words came back to her. Did he really live here out of sheer spite? Spite about what? He was utterly unfathomable. Sophie went back to her room and methodically cleared all the things that were littering the lovely blue carpet. Practical actions drove other thoughts out of her head and she soon had all her books neatly arranged in the bookcase, her possessions in the drawers. One more cupboard and she would be finished. She would ask Matthew about it at dinnertime.

She wasn't looking forward to that either. Matthew had eaten in his study at lunchtime and Sophie had eaten with Biddy in the kitchen, but there would be no escape tonight. She sighed and reached for the last of her things—a photograph of her mother and father. She sat on the carpet and looked at them closely.

It was true that her father had had the bright hair she had herself. His had been a little more fair, less burnished with fire, but he'd had her eyes, slightly lighter but still the unusual violet. Her mother's face in the photograph was beautiful but aloof—so aloof that the beauty was almost missed, and Sophie felt mournful when she realised that by now she felt nothing. She was alone.

It was almost impossible to imagine her father in this house with Matthew. He had been twelve years older. There must have been a bond, though. It was all mysterious and she was unlikely to get to the bottom of it. She was, therefore, most likely to keep putting her foot into things.

Later, as Sophie went down to dinner, she was still musing about the past—her own past and the past in this house. It was big enough, old enough to have family portraits hanging but there were none. By now she had been in all the rooms except the other bedrooms, but there had been no sign of anything that told her about the occupants of this house before Matthew.

Trembath House. The fact that Eve had told her it meant place of the grave bothered Sophie not one little bit. The dark old house intrigued and excited her. The wild, windswept surroundings excited her too, especially the crashing waves of the sea.

Matthew's dark face came into her mind but she hastily dismissed it. She was not about to start placing him in any category, which included 'intriguing' and 'exciting'. She needed no trouble at all. She would crouch quietly in her refuge and then leave hastily in September with a few well-chosen words of gratitude.

Sophie wished that the time were upon her now as she went into the dining-room and saw Matthew. Apparently he had not recovered from his burst of anger, because as she came in he stood with a drink in his hand and gave her a top-to-toe inspection with no sign of enthusiasm at all. Her feelings went from anxiety to embarrassment and finally to resentment.

She had gone to a good deal of trouble to look nice. She was wearing a warm navy blue dress with a white-spotted collar and a matching belt. The dress was a bit short because she liked to be fashionable, but she knew it suited her colouring and she had brushed her short curls until they shone like new pennies. There was no need for him to stand there staring at her so unwaveringly as if she were a freak.

'Drink, Sophie?' he finally asked when she was at the stage of feeling her face glowing with mixed anger and embarrassment. Even the way he said it was annoying—as if she should only be allowed a lemonade. She decided to cut the ground away from under his feet.

'Could I have a lemonade?' she enquired sweetly, and his dark brows shot up in astonishment before she saw that amused, twisted smile.

'Throwing down the gauntlet?' he enquired wryly. 'Was it something I said? You're not nearly as tranquil as Quentin was.'

'I probably picked up my annoying ways from my mother,' she suggested sharply, and the smile faded from his face at once.

'Her annoying ways were different,' he growled. 'I can't say that I ever found her amusing.' He handed her a drink and she discovered that it was a very nice sweet sherry. She didn't need to continue the conversation either because Biddy came in with the meal and served it from the trolley as they sat down to eat.

It seemed that being reminded of her mother had thrown Matthew back into gloom, and Sophie searched around for a way to make polite conversation when Biddy had retreated to the kitchen.

'This is a lovely old house,' she ventured, looking round at the dining-room with its damask-covered walls and expensive curtains. From this room long French windows looked out over the garden to the sea, but it was now too dark outside to see anything.

'It's been in my family for generations,' he replied shortly. 'I expect Quentin told you.'

'No, he never did. He rarely talked about Cornwall. Mostly it was the latest dig, the finds, cataloguing.' Sophie's voice was tight too and he looked up at her sharply.

'You were interested in things like that?'

'I might have been, given the chance. He talked to my mother. They were wrapped up in each other.'

'Don't you mean wrapped up in their work?' Matthew enquired drily. 'It's hard to imagine Iris being captivated by another human being.'

'You paint a very cold picture of her,' Sophie stated. The fact that he was right seemed to make no difference. She felt the primitive need to defend her mother.

'You mean I'm wrong?' he asked scathingly. 'You remember a motherly woman who cuddled you, played with you, kissed you? To my certain knowledge you were shipped off to school at five and more or less left there. Has something escaped me?'

'You—you didn't know them,' she muttered, self-pity threatening to drown her. Nothing had escaped him and she couldn't imagine anything ever escaping him. There was no need cruelly to dissect everything, though. She had pushed her hurt to the back of her mind years ago. She could cope with life very well indeed. 'Anyway, I was talking about the house.'

'But it's hard to think of a house without picturing the people in it,' Matthew assured her. 'Especially this house.' He leaned back and contemplated the rich colour of the wine in his glass. 'This house was more important to my father than any people. In fact, the people in it were simply figures that moved around like ghosts, keeping out of his way if they had any sense.' He glanced across at her and suddenly grinned. 'You would have been in serious trouble, Sophie Grant. My father would have taken a stick to you merely because of the defiant look on your face.'

'You—you didn't like him?' she asked. There had been a tone of savagery in his voice that told of dislike and it was alarming. She admitted that she had been indifferent to her parents—as indifferent finally as they had been to her—but actually to dislike——

'I hated him,' Matthew informed her flatly. 'I was five when my mother died but I remember her. I remember her beaten expression, her pale face. Looking back, I can understand that she had little to live for, not even me.'

'Your father married again—married Daddy's mother.'

'In the same year that my mother died,' he agreed. 'It was like the sun coming into the house. Your grandmother was bright, beautiful—like you. She had the same glowing hair, although her eyes were not quite so astonishing. She had room in her heart for me too. For a while life was good. I even had a big brother to follow around and he bore my presence with fortitude. I hero-worshipped Quentin and I adored your grandmother.'

'So—so what went wrong?' Sophie asked softly. She was stunned to find that Matthew was confiding in her, telling her about his life. He had seemed so steadfastly sure of himself but there was a bitterness about his voice now that spoke of a long time of hurt.

'Nothing went wrong. My father reverted to type. He married your grandmother because he needed a woman around the house, but he did not need someone who sang and laughed, who questioned his ways, and he did not need two boys who got into mischief. Quentin went off to university and I went off to boarding-school. This house was silent then, just as he liked it. His new wife was little more than a servant. Eventually, when I came home from school, I could hardly recognise her. A few years later she fell off that cliff.'

A shudder ran over Sophie's skin and she was silent. No wonder she had picked up a sort of gothic atmosphere. It was as if he had been speaking of times long, long ago.

'Why don't you get rid of the house if it has so many bad memories?' she finally blurted out, and he looked across at her sardonically.

'Maybe I want to hang around here to irritate him,' he suggested.

'You can't get your own back on somebody who's dead,' she pointed out, and his gaze sharpened intensely.

'Really? Isn't that why you ran off to London instead of going to university? Isn't that precisely why you're having to start all over again now?'

'I chose not to go right away,' she insisted stiffly. 'In any case, lots of people go later, when they've had some experience of life. I'm not too old.'

'You're a babe,' he murmured drily. 'I would say too that your experience of life is probably about sufficient to fill an eggcup. I suppose that makes it Quentin's fault but I could forgive him just about anything. A warm and willing woman would have made all the difference to his life.'

Once again he was lashing out at her mother and Sophie retaliated almost without thought, the memory of Delphine Trevelyan's cold, beautiful face in her mind.

'Is that what you found?' she enquired, and his expression changed like lightning, alarming her. She didn't know what had got into her, speaking to him like that. After all, she had never known his wife and he was probably still mourning her. 'I'm sorry,' she offered hastily. 'I really am,' she added when he just went on looking at her coldly. 'Saying that was unforgivable.'

'Oh, I know all about retaliation,' he assured her. 'Let's just say that I didn't expect it quite so quickly from you. Maybe we'd better keep off the subject of relatives.'

Sophie nodded anxiously and took a great gulp of her wine. It would be a good idea to remember who he was and who she was. It would also be a good idea to remember where she was—at his mercy. It was not until the meal was over and they were having coffee that she summoned up enough courage to ask to phone London. She didn't want to lose track of her friends.

'Consider the telephone yours,' Matthew said generously. 'Use it whenever you wish. I expect you'll need to keep in touch with the boyfriend?'

Not really. She had been considering phoning Esther but she should phone Andy too, and in any case she still felt defiant.

'Yes, I really do,' she said in a heartfelt voice, remembering his remarks about her experience and an eggcup.

'Invite him down here,' he offered in his alarming way, and all she could think to say was,

'Thank you.'

There was amusement back in his eyes, though, and that was a relief.

Sophie escaped to bed, feeling somewhat chastened. She would have to watch her tongue with Matthew Trevelyan. He was more than a match for her. In the morning she would ring Esther and maybe in the evening she would ring Andy when he was back at home. That would keep her feet on the ground. A few more smart remarks to Matthew and he would gobble her up like a dragon. Those cat-like eyes had turned icy several times today. She had probably managed to annoy him more in one day than other people did in a whole year. It was a dangerous success.

*   *   *

The sun was shining brilliantly next morning, its light filling the room as Sophie went down to breakfast, and the sign of good weather to come seemed to have lifted Biddy's spirits. She was chatting away even though Matthew was there.

'There'll be a good Easter, just you mark my words,' she predicted. 'This sort of weather at this time always stays over Easter. Anyway, it means that Master Philip will be able to get some fresh air when he gets home for half-term.'

'He's not exactly without fresh air now,' Matthew pointed out wryly. 'They get a fair amount of weather where he is.'

'Not like Port Withian,' Biddy insisted. Her face suddenly creased in smiles. 'You'll be getting him today?'

'Tomorrow,' he corrected her, but the one-day delay didn't dash her spirits.

'I'll be stocking up on scones, then.' She bustled out and Sophie sat quietly, waiting for someone to tell her what the conversation had been about. Matthew seemed to be reluctant to speak and she settled to her breakfast, not daring to pry.

'Miraculous,' he murmured drily. 'A female with no curiosity.'

'Biddy?' she enquired guilelessly, and his lips twitched in amusement.

'You're dying to know what we were talking about but you're determined not to ask,' he surmised.

'I wouldn't like to irritate you by prying,' she said stiffly. 'I haven't done too well so far. I thought it best to keep out of things.'

'That's going to take some doing, Miss Grant,' he drawled sardonically. 'Like it or not, you are part of the household, and tomorrow the other member joins us. Philip comes home from school.'

'Philip?' Sophie looked up slowly, determined not to show too much interest, but his next words drove the cool, polite expression from her face.

'Philip,' he repeated. 'My son.'

It had never occurred to Sophie that Matthew might have a child and she stared at him in confusion, not quite knowing what to say. He was not about to help and finally she managed to ask Philip's age.

'He's eight.' There was a subtle change in his expression and once again she knew that she was treading on thin ice.

'I—I'll look forward to seeing him, then. I hope he won't mind having a guest in the house.'

'He will not,' Matthew assured her firmly. 'Philip is a very obliging little chap.'

So why didn't he keep him at home, send him to a local school? Once again Sophie had questions racing through her mind and they troubled her all morning. It seemed to her that, having lost his wife, Matthew would have wanted to see more of his son and not send him away. She knew perfectly well that he still missed Delphine; it had been obvious from his expression when she had first arrived and had mentioned his marriage. Why not cling to their son, then?

Under the same circumstances she was sure that she would not have wanted the little boy out of her sight. Of course, there was Eve Corwin—*Mrs* Corwin; Sophie had not failed to note the ring on her finger. She was something of a complication; it would perhaps be awkward with Philip around. Still, not as awkward as it would be with *her* around.

Sophie grinned to herself. She was quite amused at the thought that her own presence would cramp Eve's style. Was that lady accustomed to coming to the house when Biddy left? How very trying it must be for her now.

Sophie was still amused by it when she went down into the hall later to get herself a mid-afternoon cup of tea. The sunlight was quite dazzling in the hall and she didn't notice Matthew standing at the door of his study. He was watching her, watching the way the sunlight turned her burnished curls to red fire, and as Sophie finally noticed him she stopped abruptly, encompassed by the feeling that he had been reading her rather wicked thoughts.

'Er—was there something...?' she asked guiltily.

'Nothing at all.' His expression didn't change; she still had his undivided attention, his eyes concentrating on her in an alarming manner. 'I noticed you coming down the stairs. The sunlight does wonderful things to your hair. I'm a writer, don't forget. I may want you to trip about outside while I watch.'

Sophie's face coloured prettily and her own alarm deepened. Trip about while he watched? Not likely! It was bad enough standing still while he watched. He wasn't smiling either. He was sure to be lying. He had probably got some way of reading her thoughts. Those unusual eyes could probably see through layers of concrete. They would have no difficulty in detecting malicious glee.

She made a decidedly noncommittal sound and turned to the kitchen, escape right at the front of her mind.

'By the way,' he added quietly, 'tonight we'll dine out and let Biddy go early. There's a good place in Port Withian. Eve Corwin's husband owns it; in fact they run it together. It has quite a reputation.'

As what? Sophie thought darkly. She gave him a brief nod of approval and dived for the kitchen, quite sure that she saw him grin after her in his wolfish manner. There! That just about proved that he had read her mind. It was too much of a coincidence.

'I hear we're dining out tonight, Biddy, and you're getting an early night,' she said breathlessly as she arrived full tilt in Biddy's domain.

'Am I, dear? Why, that's nice. If you're quite sure, I'll plan around it.'

'Well, Mr Trevelyan just told me,' Sophie warned. 'I don't expect he was joking but you'd better check.'

She made her cup of tea as Biddy went off to ascertain the facts, and she knew for sure that Matthew had said that right off the top of his head because he had picked up on her malevolent thoughts. The first person he would have told would have been Biddy if he hadn't decided on the spur of the moment. He was about to show her that his life would go on whether she approved or not. Well, she certainly didn't approve. The woman had a husband and they were carrying on right under his nose. Poor man. Sophie's heart bled for him.

Looking good for the evening became a great necessity, and as the time drew near she looked through her wardrobe and gave it a great deal of thought. Age and sophistication were called for and some mixing and matching would have to be done. She had no idea what sort of a place the Corwins had but she would dress up, not down. Eve had looked as if she would be immaculate even in the bath.

She had her shower and sprayed herself liberally with scent. She only had light, flowery perfume so she put plenty on. Getting her hair to look good was another problem. If the sunlight on it had stunned Matthew then she would have to make sure the lights did the same thing. She brushed it until her head ached because she was not going to look young in front of Eve Corwin.

The blouse she wanted to wear was a bit creased and she raced down to the kitchen in her dressing-gown to borrow Biddy's iron, anxiously watching the door all the time in case Matthew came in and caught her. He

didn't, but the older woman was all ready to leave as
Sophie went back to the hall on the way to her bedroom.
He was just coming out of his study to say goodbye to
Biddy and Sophie almost ran into him. As Biddy was
there she managed to pretend that she was invisible and
raced up the stairs, carrying her blouse, before he had
the chance to speak.

'Time you were off, Biddy,' Matthew pointed out. 'I'll
leave to get Philip the moment you arrive tomorrow
morning.'

'I'll be here bright and early, sir. I did a good bake
of scones this afternoon. Master Philip can't keep away
from my scones.'

'Neither can I, Biddy,' he told her. 'You're a wonder
with the scones and tonight you smell like something
from the *Arabian Nights*.'

'Go on with you, sir,' Biddy chortled. 'You know it's
Miss Sophie's perfume.'

Sophie didn't hang around to hear any more. She was
at her own door and she hurried inside, her face red
again. Had she overdone it with the perfume? Had it
just wafted delicately through the hall or had it almost
choked him? She had no idea and it was too late now
to shower it off. Matthew looked as if he was ready to
go.

She hurriedly dressed and then spent a moment
calming down. She didn't want to arrive in the hall in
a glistening heap. She had gone to a good deal of trouble
and she needed the poise to carry it off. Scurrying around
would just not do.

Her trousers were slim and elegant, chocolate-brown.
They looked like silk although they were not. A bargain,
Esther had said, and she had been right. The blouse was
an exact match and tucked in round her tiny waist perfectly. A gold belt finished it off and she had a couple
of gold bangles that her father had bought her when he

had been on a dig in Egypt. With high-heeled gold sandals the outfit was just about perfect and she looked at least thirty.

Sophie smiled at her reflection and collected a light coat. Not that she intended to put it on—it would spoil everything. Matthew would be used to film stars as his books had been filmed. She couldn't manage that but she could try to have some gloss.

It was very quiet as she went down the stairs and she had a chance to practise sophistication. She took it slowly, lingering on each step, watching the way her slender hand slid down the banister, the gold bangles catching the light. It was going to be easy, like being in a film. When she looked up Matthew was standing at the bottom of the stairs, evidently nonplussed by her antics; at least, he didn't say anything and she assumed that he had been watching her for some time while she'd practised her part.

'Er—I'm ready.' It wasn't exactly what a blasé woman of the world would have said, but his disconcerted looks quite threw her out of her act for a moment.

'So I see.' He stood there and she had no alternative but to continue down the stairs until she was at the bottom, facing him. The slight advantage of being one step up and therefore almost level with his lean height was no help at all. Normally she would have been able to duck her head but now she was pinned fast by two glittering eyes that gave her no clue at all. For all she knew he might be thinking that she was ridiculous. She certainly felt it.

'You're very beautiful, Sophie,' he complimented her quietly. 'It's a great honour to be able to escort you.'

She managed to mutter her thanks but really she felt awful, mean and utterly childish. She had dressed up to get the better of somebody he knew and actually she should have been feeling triumphant. Instead she felt very bad indeed. Matthew had asked her down here to Cornwall. He had made a place for her in his home and so far she had been nothing more than a nuisance. Now, when she had been planning to glitter and outdo his lady-friend, he was being nice to her.

She bit her lip and hoped that he had not realised what she had been intending to do. Of course, the plan was off now. If Eve Corwin's husband was so stupid that he did not know what was going on, maybe he deserved all he got. Anyway, right at this moment she was completely on Matthew's side.

There was brilliant moonlight as they stepped through the front door and Sophie paused to savour the beauty of it all—the shaded garden, the glitter of the sea. From here the sound of the waves was muted but there was still the rage about them that she had heard before. There was tranquillity in the night and the garden with the excitement and danger of the waves at a safe distance.

'Come on; you'll be cold in that thin blouse,' Matthew said as he waited for her to move.

'Isn't it lovely, though—the night, I mean? The garden is so quiet and mysterious and the sea so savage and exciting. I don't think I've ever seen anything as beautiful.'

'Just so long as you remember the savagery of the sea,' Matthew reminded her quietly, his glance following hers across the moonlit garden. 'There is often danger in beauty.'

She nodded and walked to the car.

'I know. I've read all your books.'

'Have you?' He smiled down at her as he opened the door for her. 'How flattering. Was it because of the relationship, or did you become addicted?'

'A bit of both,' she confessed ingenuously, settling herself into the car. 'I bought the first one out of curiosity because I vaguely remembered you; after that I was hooked.'

Matthew laughed and then came round to get into the car.

'You remembered me?'

'Only vaguely,' she cautioned. 'You scared me enough for it to stick in my mind. At least, it was probably my mother's words that scared me. She said you were Black Cornish.'

Oops! Sophie knew that she had once again walked into a hole. So much for sophistication; she was babbling away like a child. When she glanced anxiously across at him, though, he was smiling, his eyes on the road.

'Black Cornish? Well, I've been called worse. I'm sorry if it scared you.'

'I'm old enough to know better now,' she said briskly, pleased that he was not annoyed.

'Yes, you are,' he reminded her very softly. 'Just remember what I said, though. There's danger in almost everything—if you look for it.'

She had no real idea what he meant by that, but his tone was peculiar and it was some time before he spoke again—not, in fact, until they were in Port Withian, and by then Sophie's great daring had oozed away, together with her air of sophistication. All she felt now was well dressed. The glittering seductress was only a figment of her wild imagination. Matthew had only to lower his tone and her heart raced like a wild bird's. She had better leave the thrilling plots to him.

It was quiet in Port Withian and she wondered why this should surprise her. Of course it would be quiet. It was not the tourist season yet, and this was a small fishing village, not some big city. Even so, after the constant noise and bustle of London, the quiet and the calm hit her immediately. They parked by the harbour wall and there was nobody there at all; the whole village was silent.

'It seems to be deserted.' Her voice was uneasy, and Matthew glanced at her and then laughed in that low, dark tone she was becoming quite used to.

'Not really.' He pointed to the small pub just down the village street. The lights were shining from it on to the rounded cobbles and she could now hear voices. 'That place will be full, especially later on, and I don't expect Eve and Brad are sitting around with nothing to do. Their little place is popular. In the summer it's hard to get a table there.'

But not for him. Eve would see to it that Matthew always had a table at the establishment. So her husband was called Brad. Sophie wondered what he looked like. There was not much chance that he would look as splendid and striking as Matthew so he would have lost before he had even begun. Now that they were there her earlier feelings began to surface, and she found her mind making up pictures of Eve fluttering her lashes at Matthew right under the poor husband's nose, even in front of crowds of tourists in the summer.

The annoyance came back with a rush and she walked with some reluctance beside Matthew as he headed across the street towards a rather dark, unevenly cobbled alley.

'Come on,' he urged as she slowed considerably. 'I hope you're not thinking of making a run for the car? If anyone springs on you I promise to flatten them.'

'It's the cobbles,' she muttered. 'I'm wearing high heels.'

It was partly true anyway. At this rate she would twist an ankle and it would all end in tears.

'I noticed,' he murmured. 'You aged considerably between ironing your blouse and coming down the stairs.'

Sophie blushed in the semi-darkness. It reminded her of her clouds of perfume and his remarks about the

Arabian Nights. Was she still choking him? She drew away uneasily and he pounced on her at once.

'A few more steps and we're there,' he insisted, taking her arm in a firm grip. She was pressed to his side and it suddenly occurred to her that her perfume must be making him feel faint at such close proximity. She hadn't thought of it in the car. When they got back in there it would hit them like a venomous cloud. Sophie's face glowed with mortification.

'I'm really sorry about the perfume,' she blurted out, and he glanced down at her in astonishment.

'You're delightfully bizarre, Sophie Grant. The perfume is wonderful.'

So polite, she mused darkly. Of course, he would be, being, as he was, a famous writer and a man of the world. The compliment had probably choked him more than the perfume. 'Delightfully bizarre'! He meant mentally deranged, and she was going out of her way to prove it.

'Thank you,' she managed coolly, deciding to accept the compliment and ignore the remark about her mental state. 'I wondered if I had put on a little too much. This is such a quiet little spot and I'm more accustomed to London.'

'Oh, they've discovered perfume down here,' he murmured drily. 'It's not all clotted cream and scones.'

That was a complete put-down, of course, and Sophie felt more gauche and foolish than ever, but fortunately they had arrived at a brightly lit glass door and she was inside before she could make an even bigger fool of herself.

CHAPTER FOUR

IT WAS not exactly as Sophie had pictured it. In her mind there had been scenes of a huge, softly lit room, candles on the tables, music in the background and Eve's husband looking harassed and downtrodden as Eve wound sinuously between the tables, talking quietly to wealthy customers while her eyes strayed knowingly to Matthew.

The only thing that fitted into Sophie's mental picture was the soft music. The lights on the tables came from small, well-shaded lamps. As for the rest, it was quite a small room that they entered, and an archway, looking old enough to have been there for centuries, led into a further room.

There was a long, curving bar—again old, well polished—and the man standing behind it was not in any way harassed—at least, not as far as Sophie could see. He was tall and quite good-looking, his hair dark brown and his eyes grey. He didn't cringe at the sight of Matthew either. He looked most welcoming. Sophie knew without being told that this was Brad Corwin and he greeted Matthew with a quick grin as he came round the bar to meet them.

There was no sign of his wife, and Sophie wondered for one light-headed minute if Eve was in the kitchen with an apron round her waist and a white cap on her head as she cooked the meal. What a delightful thought that was. She perked up considerably and managed a brilliant smile as Brad came close.

'I've already heard about you, Miss Grant. Eve told me about Matt's niece Sophrina.'

'Don't irritate her,' Matthew drawled. 'She has a tendency to snap when enraged. The name is Sophie and she is *not* my niece.' He glanced round the room, which was only partly filled as yet. 'We'll have that table by the window if it's not booked. Sophie can look out at the harbour. She likes the sea.'

He turned away, taking her arm and urging her to the table he had picked out.

'Drinks?' Brad asked, and Matthew nodded.

'Sherry. Make mine dry; Sophie likes hers sweet.'

He had no idea about that, she mused angrily. He had only seen her drink sherry once and for all he knew she might have just been being polite.

She wouldn't have been having these mutinous thoughts, she realised, if he hadn't been so proprietorial, if he hadn't treated her like an adolescent. He had not given her one moment with Brad Corwin. He had simply seized her arm and marched her off. So much for lingering at the bar and getting to know the man who would need an ally very soon, unless Eve was knee-deep in cooking, her well-groomed head in some huge, hot oven.

'You can sit here.' Matthew held her chair and left her no choice, and Sophie slid elegantly into her seat, the elegance somewhat marred by the fact that she still had her coat clutched in her arms.

Matthew took it firmly from her.

'I'll get rid of this for you,' he offered. 'I'd quite forgotten that you had it. Why didn't you put it on? It's not too warm outside.'

'It doesn't go with the outfit,' she muttered, reddening as he observed her with those curious cat-like eyes. His smile grew slowly as he looked down at her.

'You could have kept the outfit a secret until we got here,' he suggested. 'Much more of an impact that way.'

'I don't try to make impacts,' she assured him stiffly, her cheeks beginning to glow even more hotly under the inflexible golden stare.

'You've already made one with Brad,' he murmured sardonically. 'He'll be falling over his feet to get the sherry here.'

'What a terrible thing to say,' she gasped. 'He seems to be a very nice, polite man, and he was friendly because he had been forewarned and obviously thought I was related to you.'

'Of course!' Matthew snapped his fingers theatrically. 'Why didn't I think of that? It explains it all.' He looked down at her in a sceptical manner and went off to dispose of her coat, leaving her staring after him with a bewildered and embarrassed expression on her face. Now what was he up to?

It didn't take her long to fathom it out. He was putting her at a disadvantage so that she would sit like a mouse when he had the chance to talk to Eve. She sat back and smiled smugly. It was all for the best because it had put her right back on her mettle. She would stick to him like glue. A tenacious look came to her face and she glanced across to see him talking to Brad as if nothing untoward had happened at all.

How very cynical. Did Brad have no idea or did he just accept things? Men were quite deceitful creatures. She spared Andrew a warm blessing. It was, after all, best to stick to her own age-group. She had felt completely in control there. With Matthew she was not at all sure. He went from being kind and friendly to being harsh and icy, and in between he managed to read her mind and look at her with sardonic detachment. It would be interesting to see how he behaved towards his son.

'Do you have far to go to collect Philip?' she asked later as they sipped their drinks and waited for the meal they had ordered.

'Not too far. In any case, you'll see for yourself. I'm taking you with me.'

There it was again, this *attitude*. Sophie looked at him primly.

'It's kind of you to offer,' she assured him coolly, 'but I'm not sure if I——'

'You're dying to go, Sophie. You go to great trouble not to pry but your mind probes into everything. Besides,' he added as she looked aggrieved and sought for some cutting remark to devastate him, 'it will give you a chance to see something of the West Country and a chance to get to know Philip before we get back to the house.'

She nodded in agreement and murmured her thanks. She noted that he had not said 'home'. Always Trembath was 'the house'. She was still mulling things over when their meal arrived, with, hard on its heels, Eve Corwin, who had definitely not been in any oven, even by a fingertip. The perfect grooming was intact and she homed in on Matthew like a bird of prey, which to Sophie's mind was exactly what she was.

'Darling! You brought your niece!'

She came across and put her hand familiarly on his shoulder and Sophie was startled at the burst of anger that shot through her. It was quite ridiculous and she knew that perfectly well. Eve and Matthew were at the very least old friends, while she had only been here in Cornwall for a short time. Even so, it was an intrusion, because in that time Sophie had begun to feel curiously safe with him.

'Sophie is not my niece,' Matthew pointed out with slightly bored amusement. 'You'd better learn that, Eve.

I notice you passed on the erroneous information to Brad.'

'Well, there's a sort of relationship, and it's such a bore to begin an explanation about your stepbrother and his wife and then Sophrina. Much more simple to tell everyone that she's your niece.'

'I would have thought it much more simple to let people mind their own business,' he murmured. 'Too much interest and we'll simply have to eat at the house each night.'

Sophie glanced at him quickly. He seemed slightly rattled. It was intriguing. It even made her forget that Eve had deliberately called her Sophrina. She only realised how much she was staring when Matthew raised his head and quirked an eyebrow at her. Eve was watching both of them with some suspicion and Sophie quickly ducked her head and got on with her meal.

They were not to be left in peace, apparently, because almost at once Brad arrived, ostensibly to see if everything was all right but clearly in fact to check up on his wife.

'And how is our beautiful visitor enjoying her meal?' he asked, in the sort of voice that set Sophie's teeth on edge.

'Ask her. She has a limited command of English.' Matthew's pithy remark brought a flush to Sophie's cheeks and a smile of satisfaction to Eve's face.

'The food is very good.' Sophie summoned up her most husky voice, remembering Matthew's words. 'I was a little surprised when Matthew said we were eating out. Biddy's cooking is wonderful, but I can see that this makes a nice change and it does give her a night off.'

'So we don't measure up to Biddy?' Brad sounded amused and Sophie shook her head, looking thoughtful.

'Oh, I never said that. It's just that I'm content to stay at home. You probably have things on the menu that Biddy wouldn't tackle. I never got the chance to find out. Matthew ordered for me.' She produced the husky voice again as she said his name and she was gleefully aware that this was not going down well at all with Eve. She was not too pleased, though, to see the effect this was having on Brad. His expression was one of amused indulgence, as if she were a child. Men of that age were apparently all the same.

At the moment she didn't exactly know whose side she was on except that it was definitely not Eve's. Matthew went on eating, looking up at her from beneath dark brows every time she made a statement. As for Brad, Sophie was not entirely sure that she liked him, downtrodden or not.

'Do you do the cooking?' she asked, with a pleasant smile of enquiry on her face as she looked at Eve.

'I do not!' It was enough to send Eve on her way, and as Brad left he was laughing quietly to himself.

Not bad for an opening skirmish. Sophie gave a little sigh of satisfaction and went back to eating. It was a bit like having made a good strike at bowling—people flying off in all directions. Eve was now busy charming another couple, and as Sophie's eye strayed in her direction Matthew put his knife and fork down and regarded her steadily.

'Are you working to some sort of plan or was that your usual dinnertime conversation?'

His voice was lazily enquiring but there was just an edge of annoyance in it and Sophie looked up unflinchingly, ready to tackle him head-on.

'Did I say something wrong? I merely answered when spoken to.'

'Is that what it was? I really must be there when you have an argument. It will certainly be worth my while to listen.'

'Well, if you must know, I don't like either of them!' It was no use beating about the bush, and she threw down the gauntlet with an expression of cool indifference on her face.

'You're not obliged to like them,' he reminded her coldly. 'The Corwins are *my* friends.'

'*Both* of them?' It was out before Sophie could stop it and it gained her the most hostile look that Matthew had given her so far. For several seconds he stared at her, his eyes an icy gold. If Sophie had been nervous she would have run right out of the room, but she held her ground.

'Keep out of my affairs, Sophie,' he said in a quiet yet harsh voice.

'I—I'm not interested in your affairs.' The temptation to add more was uppermost but there was something about his expression that told her to hold her tongue.

'I sincerely hope not. Life will go on as before when you are away from here and cosily settled at university. Meanwhile, you skirt on the very edge of things. Remember that.'

It was the end of any sort of conversation and Sophie was no longer hungry. She had antagonised Matthew because of her inability to leave well alone. The chance of being forgiven was remote. And all for some man she didn't even like and some woman who irritated her.

What Matthew did with his life was nothing to do with her at all. He probably had women-friends all over the world. He probably had somebody really special in America. None of this was any of her business; in fact, she couldn't really understand why she had taken such an attitude, or even any attitude at all.

Instead of going when the meal was finished, they ended up at the bar. Matthew had another drink and ordered one for her.

'Please, I'm not used to drinking,' she muttered anxiously, afraid of offending him further. He just ignored her, but when the drinks came she was relieved to see that hers was a lime and lemon. She had been so agitated that she hadn't even heard him change the order.

He intended to snub her anyhow. That was quite clear because he got into conversation with a few local people and she was ignored. She looked steadfastly away when Brad looked in her direction and Eve was much too busy laughing and joining in, her eyes constantly on Matthew.

'Aren't you going to introduce your friend?'

One woman was finally unable to contain her curiosity and Matthew had no time to reply before Eve said, 'Sophie Grant. She's staying with Matt.' It was said with a good deal of malice, meant to embarrass, and as far as Sophie was concerned it succeeded. Matthew wasn't helping out at all. He was enjoying this as much as Eve, and Sophie felt her face beginning to burn.

'We're—er—related...' she began.

'But only by the past,' Matthew insisted, his voice quite loud enough to be heard. 'It's wonderful having Sophie around. Biddy dotes on her.'

'Who wouldn't?' Brad interjected, and although she could see that this had all backfired on Eve Sophie wished herself miles away. Too many eyes were on her, too many expressions were speculating, but the eyes that she dreaded most were watching her like a vengeful cat's.

People began to talk to her. In fact, there was a sudden rush of conversation which Sophie knew was a cover for embarrassment. She couldn't remember later one word that had been said or how she had answered, but when Matthew suddenly appeared at her side with her coat held out for her she was almost ready to scream with rage and humiliation.

'Time to go.' He looked at her closely and her lips tightened, partly with annoyance but most of all to stop them trembling with self-pity.

'See you soon, Sophie.' Brad managed to make his voice heard and Eve looked daggers at them both. She quite obviously wanted both Matthew and her own husband. It sickened Sophie and she tried to turn away.

'Say goodnight, Sophie.' Matthew's arm came tightly round her shoulders, the force of his grip making her face the bar and the still interested eyes. His voice was a low murmur, for her ears only, and Sophie forced herself to produce a rather weak smile as she said goodnight. 'There. You managed that beautifully,' he taunted softly. 'A few more trips out and we'll have you quite civilised.'

He kept his arm round her and she endured it until they were back in the cobbled alley that led to the harbour and the car. Then she pulled free and turned to glare up at him, her eyes dark with anger in the lights from the restaurant windows.

'I suppose you think it was funny to humiliate me?' she snapped. 'I suppose you feel good about it?'

'Not particularly,' he assured her coldly. 'I wondered if you would get the point that rumours are easily started.'

'I have no idea what you're talking about.'

She spun away and set off at a brisk, military march to the car, uncertain whether or not just to pass it and walk to Trembath alone. Only the thought of the dark drive and the equally dark bushes prevented her.

She knew exactly what he was talking about. She had made a fool of herself and Matthew had assisted and then paid her back. But it seemed to her that he had paid her back very harshly and she was raging inside, quite ready to do grievous harm to anyone who stopped her. Fate kept them safe, however, because not only was the village deserted but the cobbles of the main street attacked her in a vicious way and had her losing her balance before she was halfway across the road.

Sophie gave a little squeal as she felt herself slipping and an iron-strong arm lashed round her waist and caught her, lifting her until her feet were off the ground and out of danger.

'Put me down!' she gasped, glaring into Matthew's face.

'And have you sprain an ankle? We've already had you in bed since you came here. Biddy has other things to do with her time. I'll put you down when we're safely at the car.' Two long strides and they were there and she was deposited on her feet.

'I'm not going back to Trembath House!' she snapped. 'I'll find a place to stay here in the village and in the morning I'll go back to London.'

'You little lunatic.' He opened the car door and thrust her inside. 'I've had more than enough of your deranged company for one evening.' He got into the car and slammed the door then started the engine. 'One more word,' he threatened, 'and I'll put you across my knee.'

'You wouldn't dare! There are laws——'

'And a whole restaurant of people who think you've simply moved in with me. I imagine I'd get a lenient sentence.'

Sophie was silent, dumbfounded by this alien logic.

'You—you know they don't think that,' she managed at last. 'They knew it was a—a joke.'

'I doubt it.' His brief remark made everything seem so terribly serious and she panicked.

'Eve will tell them!' She blurted the words out and he glanced at her coldly as the car left the village and headed for the steep climb by the cliffs.

'Mrs Corwin to you, child. She is not very likely to say anything. She started the rumour if you recall. Besides, it suits her for some reason.'

'You know the reason!' she accused, and he nodded unconcernedly.

'That's right. I do. Now, if you can manage to keep silent I'll be grateful.'

As she was too horrified to speak Sophie had no trouble at all in keeping silent, and she watched the dark countryside and listened to the wild sound of the sea as her mind turned over the enormity of her evening out.

Matthew kept silent too, and it was not until the car had stopped outside the front door of Trembath House that he glanced at her again, his keen eyes noting her pale, distressed face.

'Of course,' he remarked casually, 'knowing Eve and her ways, she has probably already told half the village that I'm looking after my niece. That being the case, nobody is likely to take much notice of her latest remarks, especially as Biddy lives amongst them and has taken you under her wing. I would think that your reputation is still snow-white.'

Sophie stared at him, feelings flooding through her like the colours of the rainbow. He was quite right and she knew it. He had robbed her of her common sense earlier and he had made her suffer because she had dared to answer back when those two had sniped at her. He had enjoyed seeing her squirm and now he was coolly setting things right.

'You—you miserable...!' She turned on him furiously but he caught her raised fists before they could find their mark.

'Sophie! Sophie!' he exclaimed with mocking despair. 'I really must spare some time to tame you. I can see that you'll be a very bad influence on Philip. Tomorrow you'll have to behave a good deal better than this.'

'I'm not going!' She pulled free and got out of the car, glaring at him as he got out the other side and watched her with cool interest. 'I'm not going with you to get your son, and when you get back I'll be long gone!'

She stormed off into the house, noting that the door had been left unlocked. Villains could be in there waiting to attack her for all he knew. It would amuse him, no doubt. Her mind went back to his books and she decided that she was not one bit surprised by his behaviour. Only a scoundrel could write books like that.

Tomorrow she would pack and get back to London somehow. She would have to throw herself on somebody's mercy but it would be a good deal safer than the mercy she was getting here. Matthew Trevelyan managed to get her into a turmoil with ease and she could not afford to allow it.

Next morning Sophie stood at the bedroom window and viewed the sea. It was a beautiful day. The wild Cornish sea was almost tranquil, a blue sky casting deeper blue shadows in the troughs of the gentle waves. It really was lovely here and it would get more lovely as the summer advanced.

She looked across the lawns to the cliff-edge. There was an added gloss to the leaves of the rhododendron bushes and for once the trees were still, no longer at war with the wind. A thoughtful look came to her face. In London it would be very different, and what could she hope for? Matters were exactly the same as when she had left to come down here. Matters were worse, actually.

The few pieces of second-hand furniture that she and Esther had gathered had been sold and every other thing she owned was with her here, right in this room. Esther was now in the nurses' home, safe until she married, and she had sounded happy when Sophie had phoned her. Andy was happy too, getting on with his course, and there was probably another girl to catch his eye. More than any of this, though, Sophie had sung the praises of Trembath and Matthew Trevelyan very loudly indeed.

If she went back she would have to face the fact that she had made a hasty judgement which had turned out to be wrong. Also, there was the little matter of cash. She didn't have any, or, at least, not enough to see her through.

She bit her lip as she saw Matthew come into the garden on his way back after that morning swim he always took. The wet towel was there again, his hair was gleaming in the sunshine, and she felt an odd quiver of alarm when she found her mind dwelling on the lithe way he walked, the clear-cut lines of his face and the way his firm lips were twisted in a half-smile.

Sophie turned away quickly. She was rapidly digging a hole for herself. She had already behaved like a fool and now she would have to announce that she had decided to stay after all. She paced around the room for a few seconds and then straightened up determinedly. Better to face him now and get it over with, although, after the way she had behaved last night and the way she had stormed into the house and off to bed, if he stared at her in his devastating way and told her to pack her things she wouldn't really blame him.

It would have been better if he had been a grouchy old man with a lined, weather-beaten face. Step-uncles were supposed to be like that. It was just typical of her luck that she had been landed with the splendid Matthew Trevelyan. No doubt some sullen deity was watching with interest, paying her back for one of her many faults. She probably *was* Wednesday's child. She would have to look it up.

She gave Matthew another second to drop his wet towel on the polished chair and then went down. If he threw her out she would at least eat her breakfast first and

Biddy would probably pack her a lunch. It would see her through the day and she would only have to worry about the next six months.

He was already having breakfast when she arrived and he didn't say good morning, which was an unnerving sign. Instead he looked at her steadily for a second and then stood to hold her chair for her.

'Good morning,' Sophie managed breathlessly. 'Sorry if I'm late.'

'Are you? I never noticed.' He sat opposite and returned to his meal. 'We're in no great hurry. Philip isn't free to leave until just before lunchtime.'

'Philip?' She looked at him blankly. Had he forgotten her outburst? Had it failed to register in his mind that she was leaving today?

'Philip,' he agreed, not even bothering to glance at her. 'We're collecting him this morning. Surely you hadn't forgotten?'

'I—I—but I said I was leaving today...' She stared at him anxiously but he still continued to eat.

'And you changed your mind,' he pointed out. 'That puts us back to the original plan.'

'How—how do you know I changed my mind?' she wanted to know, and he actually bothered to look up then, although when she saw his expression she rather wished he had not. His cat-like eyes were gleaming as he stared at her unwaveringly.

'An assumption,' he informed her. 'You arrived for your breakfast in a sensible manner. You do not appear to be either huffy or sulky, so we seem to be back where we were.'

'I don't sulk,' she muttered, looking quickly at her plate when his eyes took on an added gleam that she knew was amused malice. 'I'm being polite. As a guest here I——'

'You also look a little anxious,' he continued softly, ignoring her explanation. 'Once again, I forgive you, Sophie. You will stay here until you leave for university. This morning we will collect Philip. Other than that, there is nothing to discuss. Do not, however, spoil my day with any further tantrums.'

'I'm neither a child nor an idiot!' His attitude of weary tolerance stung her into a sharp reply and he cast her a look of extreme impatience.

'You're depressingly young. It probably accounts for your faults. Now eat your breakfast and let's be off.'

Sophie was fuming but she managed to control herself, though how long that would last she didn't like to speculate. She was not sure if he was goading her or being naturally superior. Either way she couldn't last out long and she knew it.

She was glad of her change of plan, however, when they left the house and drove down to Port Withian. She glanced back at Trembath House and felt a surge of pleasure at the sight of its stone walls, the way it stood against the sunlit sky and watched the sea. In many ways, although she had been slightly unnerved at her first sight of it, Trembath House was the place of her dreams.

She had never really considered the place where her father had lived so her feelings for it were not due to any homing instinct. Maybe it had somehow crept into Matthew's books; maybe it coloured his outlook and had transmitted itself to her, because she had to admit that she had read his books over and over. She gave a sigh that was almost contentment and he glanced across at her, noting the direction of her gaze.

'Behave yourself and I might give you the house,' he said quietly. It was lightly said, but there was again a slight edge to his voice and Sophie spun round to look at him.

'That's an odd thing to say,' she remonstrated. 'It's not even remotely true either, and you know it.'

'Why not? Quentin lived there. If everything had been normal it would have been his home as well as mine.'

'I don't see why it should. It wasn't his father, after all.'

'It was his mother,' Matthew insisted rather grimly. 'All she got out of the marriage was misery.'

'Why don't you leave it, sell it, burn it down?' she asked in an exasperated voice. He was taking the sunlight out of the morning, and when she glanced back again she was not at all surprised to see that clouds had gathered and the house was now looking gloomy. 'Quite obviously you hate being there. I can't understand why you stay. And don't tell me it's to get your own back, because I don't believe you. You're too clever to think such idiotic thoughts.'

She glanced across at him crossly and his eyes slanted over her in an oddly speculative manner that brought her outburst to an abrupt end. Her tongue was running away with her again. She could appreciate that quite clearly.

'Do you arrange the lives of everyone you know, or have you just doggedly picked on me?' he enquired drily. 'How on earth is your boyfriend managing to function without your assistance?'

'He—he's very businesslike,' Sophie assured him hastily, pushing Andy's lighter-than-air attitude right to the back of her mind. Right now she needed someone to hide behind and as she could only use Andy she used him briskly. 'Andrew and I are very much alike. We have the same outlook.'

'Fortunate,' Matthew muttered sardonically. 'Otherwise you would be permanently covered in bruises. I believe I suggested that you kept out of my affairs. Let's make it much more clear, shall we? It's an order.'

'But surely your attitude is not good and Philip——'
She stopped with a gasp of fright as Matthew brought
the car to a halt right in the middle of the road and
turned on her furiously.

'Don't meddle with my son!' he grated harshly. 'You're
here for Quentin's sake and I wanted you to be here for
your own sake too, but say anything, do anything to
upset Philip and I'll personally take you to London and
dump you on the boyfriend with all your boxes and cases.
Do you hear me, Sophrina?'

'I hear you.' He was angry enough to make her feel
scared and right at that moment she didn't feel like protesting at his use of the hated name or pointing out that
if he took this attitude she would walk out anyway.

Sophie set her lips tightly, and with a low growl of
annoyance he started the car and continued out of the
village. Which was just as well. The place was not quite
so deserted this morning and several interested pairs of
eyes were being turned in their direction. She was glad
when the car climbed out of the village on the twisting
road, and she didn't look back again at Trembath House
even though she knew she would be able to see it standing
proudly on the opposite headland.

She had been put firmly in her place and for the
moment she had no drop of defiance left in her. It came
from being at someone's mercy and, in any case, honesty
made her admit that she had asked for it. She hadn't
been in Cornwall more than a few days and already she
was telling Matthew what he should do.

She turned her face away and gazed steadfastly out
of the window. It was utterly ridiculous that she should
feel so strongly about his affairs. What she needed was
a good talking-to from Esther but Sophie hadn't even
bothered to phone her again. Somehow life had become
exciting and London hardly ever came into her mind.

CHAPTER FIVE

THE SEA was soon left behind and once they were out from the high-banked lanes Sophie was able to look about and appreciate the countryside. The alien look she had found daunting on her way down was still there but it was now tempered by knowledge. She no longer felt herself to be a stranger in a strange place. It was partly because she now knew about her father in this remote part of England, and his life here seemed to have been more odd than any of the places he had visited for his work.

Lingering at the back of her mind was a haunting picture of her grandmother, bright hair blown by the wind from the sea, her skirts billowing behind her as she gazed out across the tossing grey-green water. Always too there was the house—Trembath. It came and went in her mind like a phantom from the past—sometimes real and bright with sunlight, echoing to the sound of Matthew's voice, sometimes dark, shadowed, a place of secrets and unhappiness. She realised that she almost felt sorry for the house itself, as if it had been let down, stranded on the cliff with only memories.

Sophie grunted irritably and pulled herself firmly into the present. It was Matthew who really got to her—with his dark, brooding looks, the way he drove and said nothing, irritation etched across his face, the tawny eyes narrowed against the sun.

She shot him a resentful glance and he seemed to know without even looking at her.

'We'd better make our peace before we see Philip,' he suggested coolly. 'He does not need two stony-faced people waiting to greet him.'

Sophie could quite imagine that it was all her fault. His aloof tone implied it. Presumably he was waiting for an abject apology.

'I'm sorry if I interfered with your affairs,' she managed in a hostile little voice. 'I'll see it doesn't happen again.'

'I'll try to believe you.' His cold manner changed to mockery. 'That being the case, we'll have coffee at the next place we see.'

She went through that carefully, looking for insult, but as none was detectable she made herself relax and worked hard at getting into a happy, easy state of mind. At least the scenery was beautiful, the rocky coast giving way to pretty, tidy villages, and finally Matthew stopped the car outside a small old inn, the front brightened by dark, weathered barrels filled with spring flowers.

'This will do.' He got out and came round to her but she was already out of the car, her eyes scanning the front of the old building with some awe.

'It looks like a suspicious place,' she ventured, and Matthew's laugh was all amusement.

'It's respectable,' he assured her. 'No doubt we would have passed by hastily in olden days but it's safe now.'

'Smugglers?' Sophie's wide-eyed question had him pausing to look down at her.

'Probably, if you believe everything the landlord tells you. He gives it a grizzly reputation to attract tourists, but as it was certainly on the route they would have taken from the coast it might all be true.'

'Gosh!' Her eyes opened even wider and he put his arm across her shoulders, urging her to the door.

'You're the story-teller's dream come true, ready to believe anything if it's romantic.'

'Or gruesome,' she added quickly. 'I'm not really gullible, however,' she finished vigorously. It was a little disconcerting to have Matthew's arm around her shoulders and she would have liked to pull away but she knew better. She already understood how swiftly his mockery could turn to wrath and she was not about to chance it right now.

'Did I suggest you were gullible?' he murmured ironically. 'How can you be gullible when you're so capable of arranging other people's lives?'

'We were not going to talk about that!' she snapped, pulling away from his arm and giving him a small, potent glare. 'There's a truce if you recall.'

'Of course there is,' he agreed. 'How did it slip my mind?'

This time he took her hand firmly and she had no alternative but to head for the inn and the coffee he had promised. He was ridiculing her. It was obvious, and she had a great urge to return to battle, but the feel of the strong, warm hand enclosing hers made the irritation drain away. She glanced down at their clasped hands, feeling her cheeks grow pink.

It was nothing like the way Andy held her hand. She wasn't sure if he was treating her like a child. He probably was but she had a crazy impulse to tighten her fingers around his and see him smile down at her. She resisted the impulse but she was glad when they reached the door and he ushered her inside, his hand falling away. It would be quite easy to become too attached to Matthew. Each day she could understand more and more why that woman Eve was enslaved.

The thought brought a sharp dig of anger and she tripped on the uneven floor in the dim light of the inn, quite relieved when Matthew caught her. This time he kept a firm hold of her arm.

'You need looking after, Sophie Grant,' he said in a low voice, and she was glad of the dim light. What she needed was a psychiatrist—fast.

As she had half expected, the landlord came across as they were having coffee and began to regale them with tales of long ago. Many of them were rather blood-thirsty and probably quite untrue, but Sophie listened with wide-eyed interest until she noticed Matthew watching her with amusement. Gullible, that was what she was—his expression said it all.

'Well, you don't look quite so woebegone,' he remarked as they emerged later into the sunlight. 'Stopping there was obviously one of my better ideas.'

'I realise he was making most of that up,' she retaliated haughtily. 'All the same, he's a good story-teller. I like listening to stories.'

'Remind me at bedtime,' Matthew drawled. 'I'll tuck you up with a good tale.'

'It would probably make my skin crawl,' she snapped, not liking his patronising manner, and he gave a very theatrical sigh.

'How tragic,' he murmured. 'I was beginning to think you liked me, and all I do is make your skin crawl.'

'I meant your frightening stories—I meant your books—I meant...' Sophie's voice trailed away as she looked up. He was standing with the car door open for her, a tilted grin on his face, and she blushed bright red before she dived for the safety of the car. Once again she had made herself look a fool. It came from trying to pit her wits against a master.

'Maybe it would be better if I didn't speak,' she muttered as he got in beside her.

'Safer,' he agreed amiably. 'Disappointing, though. I'm thinking of turning you into a new book.'

That made her annoyed. Having read his work, she knew full well that there could not be any page in a Matthew Trevelyan book that would accommodate her.

'I'm not alarming enough,' she sniffed, and he glanced across at her quickly, his golden eyes making a lightning foray over her face.

'In your own, small way,' he murmured, 'you're very alarming indeed.'

He started the car and said nothing else. Neither did Sophie. She was busy trying to fathom that one out and she still had not succeeded when they came to high, stone walls that evidently hid a huge estate of some kind.

'We've arrived,' Matthew informed her quietly. 'This is Philip's school.' He turned the car in at high wrought-iron gates and something inside Sophie's stomach lurched at the sight of the huge building that became visible across wide stretches of parkland. It had obviously been a stately home in the past, but it was more than obvious, even without Matthew's words, that it was now a school. The very air of the place screeched 'school' at her and her lips tightened automatically.

Not that it looked at all like the school where she had spent so much of her lonely life. She would have been able to sense it even in darkness, though. It might have been luxurious-looking, expensive-looking, there might even have been an air of tranquillity about it, and there certainly was, but it was school—children with no parents close by—and her heart bled for the little boy she had not even met. How could Matthew leave him here?

'Well? What do you think of it?' He looked across at her and was clearly determined to get some reaction.

'It's big,' she observed in a flat voice. Actually, it was making her toes curl just to look at it and she was already on Philip's side even if he should turn out to be a small, ugly monster.

'Never give up, do you?' There was a touch of anger in Matthew's voice and as far as Sophie could see she had done nothing to deserve it at that moment. Not that it mattered; her eyes were reluctant to leave the rather awe-inspiring view of the school.

'Normally no!' she snapped, and that seemed to be the end of any sort of conversation because when they pulled into the car park at the side of the school Matthew got out, leaned against the car and ignored her. He was probably not allowed into the building unless invited by the headmaster on special days, she mused frustratedly. That would be about par for the course. Philip would be a stiff and edgy child, exactly what she would have been herself but for her ability to be mutinous and insubordinate at all times.

Children were now coming out to the cars and Sophie opened the car door and went to stand beside Matthew. If Philip's homecoming was to be a let-down to him then it wasn't going to be because of her. Matthew continued to ignore her until a little boy with astonishingly fair hair came round the corner and grinned, his face changing and taking on a rather intrigued look as he noticed that Sophie was definitely one of the reception committee.

'Philip,' Matthew announced softly, and she was stunned. It took all her self-restraint not to draw back and look up at Matthew and then turn again to compare him with his son. There was no resemblance at all.

'How—how wonderfully fair...' she managed to stammer but he seemed content to ignore her.

'Exactly like his mother,' he murmured in that same soft voice. 'Delphine was very fair.'

Sophie knew that. She remembered all too well, and in that moment she understood why Philip had to be away at school. Matthew was still so much in love with his dead wife that he could not bear to see the resemblance between mother and son. It hurt too much so Philip had to go away.

She felt unutterably sad, gloomy and downcast. She didn't understand why but it was there all the same. Right at this moment Delphine Trevelyan seemed to be imprinted on her mind, overriding everything else, but as Philip came forward she saw a bright and smiling little boy—a boy who very obviously missed his father—and her gloom vanished because she also saw something else at the back of those eyes—a faint wistfulness—and she was back into her own schooldays with ease and back into a temper with a rush.

What did it matter how Matthew felt about Delphine? She was dead! Philip was alive and he was suffering quietly. Somehow she must put a stop to this. She opened her mouth, but even though he didn't even glance at her Matthew's hand came like a steel clamp to her arm.

'Beware how you greet your small cousin, Sophie Grant,' he warned coldly.

'He is not... and I am not...!' she began stormily, but the hand tightened considerably until she winced and Matthew's voice still dripped ice.

'Remember that when you are gone his life will still continue smoothly. Do not attempt to interfere. Ships that pass in the night would be a good picture to keep at the front of your mind.'

Sophie snatched her arm away, grunting in annoyance and rubbing at it vigorously. 'Ships that pass in the night'! They certainly did and he would do well to remember that some of them were well-armed warships! She glared up at him but all she got in response was one raised black brow as he contemplated her icily, and then he turned back to Philip who was hurrying over, looking extremely interested.

'You're Sophie,' he proclaimed, his bright blue eyes scanning her face and hair. 'You're staying with us at

Trembath. Dad wrote to me so I was all ready for you. You're lovely. Your hair looks as if it's on fire.'

'It probably is,' Matthew murmured sarcastically. 'Let's get started,' he added in a louder voice, and Sophie recovered from being flustered and smiled brightly at Philip.

'I'll sit in the back,' she announced. 'Then you can sit with your father and——'

'Oh, I like to sit in the back,' Philip stated seriously. 'It's better because I fiddle about a lot.'

'Which is only the truth,' Matthew observed drily. 'Sorry, my lady, you're stuck with me.' He opened the door for her with a very cynical look on his face, fixing her with his inflexible and penetrating golden gaze when she looked defiant. She got in, and as Philip threw himself on to the back seat Matthew loaded his things into the boot and came round to get them started. He seemed to be holding a lot of aces, Sophie mused—probably more than were in the pack.

And who would have thought that he would have written to Philip about her? Who would have thought that he would have written to Philip at all, for that matter? Maybe she was missing something here? She cast a sly glance at Matthew but he was manoeuvring them out of the parking space and she couldn't tell a thing from his expression.

After a few comments to his father Philip buried his head into a comic which he pulled out from beneath his school pullover and nothing was said as they sped back along the way they had come. There seemed to be nothing openly wrong with the boy and, try as she might, Sophie could not detect any atmosphere between Matthew and his son. There had been that look in the eyes, though, and she knew she was not mistaken. Something was making Philip unhappy and she could only assume that it was the school.

After a while Philip put aside his comic and leaned forward to gain Matthew's attention. 'Are we stopping for a snack?'

'Do I dare do otherwise? A snack it is, although Biddy has been baking for two days, since she knew you were coming back. Still, I don't suppose we can pass the usual place.'

'The usual place, then.' Philip sat back with a grin on his face and Sophie knew that whatever was wrong it was not something between Philip and his father. They even had old haunts that they frequented, and she fell to musing that if she had not been there another companion might very well have been accompanying Matthew to fetch his son home.

At least her own presence had put Eve Corwin's nose out of things. Not that being pushy would do Mrs Corwin any good at all. Matthew was still in love with his wife. She sighed and looked out of the window at the countryside. What a muddle people made of their lives, and she was no exception.

'Cheer up. Why the big sigh?' Matthew asked quietly. 'Philip and I promise not to be a burden, and if you're very good I'll let you play with him when we stop for the snack.'

'I'm not a child, Matthew,' she said seriously, glancing up at his arrogant profile. 'I've been a woman for a long time.'

'I know. I especially know when you use that husky voice.' He shot a quick glance at her, his tawny eyes skimming her face. 'Maybe I'm just a born tormentor.'

She looked away. He was all of that, and her instinct to fly at him when he mocked her had to be controlled otherwise one day she would do it, and she was sure that she would come off a very bad second.

Her anxious musing stopped as they pulled into the car park of a quaint little place, nothing at all like the small inn they had stopped at on the way. It looked like a cottage but a quick inspection assured Sophie that it was a café serving tea, scones and sandwiches and she couldn't quite understand why Philip had suddenly become very animated.

She found out when he leapt from the car and opened her door with every sign of impatience.

'Come on, Sophie,' he urged excitedly. 'This is a great place and I want to show you things before we leave.'

He was off at once, dragging her by the hand, and she looked up in a startled way to see Matthew watching both of them, a quirky smile on his dark face.

'Enjoy yourselves, children,' he advised mockingly, his eyes on Sophie. 'I'll order tea and scones for when you're quite played out.'

'Take no notice,' Philip advised, dragging her along to the high hedges that marked the boundary of the parking area. 'Dad loves to tease. It means he likes you. If he didn't he wouldn't tease. He can be quite nasty when he wants.'

'To you?' she pried quickly, but it only brought out further laughter.

'Course not! He's my dad. I don't get all my own way, though,' he added softly, his brightness dying for a minute. Sophie noted that well. She could quite imagine what Philip wanted and what was denied. He wanted to be at home and the answer would always be no. Well, she would have to see about that!

The sight that met her as they rounded the hedge took all speculation from her mind. It was like stepping into an enchanted world where everything had shrunk.

'It's a miniature town,' Philip told her excitedly as she looked at the perfect church, the houses, the stream and the roads of a Cornish town as it would have been many years ago. 'I could stay all day in this place. It's my favourite stopping-spot.'

Sophie could quite see why and they were very soon on their hands and knees, crawling round and peering into exact replicas of houses. A plaque informed her that the town had been built by the present owner's great-grandfather and that he had worked on it for twenty years, which was not surprising as everything was perfect from the tiles on the roofs to the clock on the church.

'All it needs is people,' Philip mused. 'I try to imagine myself in the town, walking down the streets. Nobody seems to know if it's a real place or if it was made up. When we go out Dad and I look at towns and try to see if any of them look like this but we haven't found the place yet. We once thought it was Launceston but it's not. No castle.'

'Does he usually come in here with you?' she asked, and Philip looked at her in a very grown-up way, almost pityingly, as if she were slightly lacking in intelligence.

'Of course,' he assured her gently. 'He likes it. He's letting you come today, though. He's like that—kind.' He thought for a minute and then added, 'He's got a terrible temper, though. Do you like him?'

'He—he's been very good to me,' she hedged, feeling unusually agitated. 'He's letting me stay until September.'

Like Matthew? Of course she liked Matthew. To try to deny it would simply be fooling herself.

'Then what?' Philip wanted to know, sitting back on his heels and giving her the benefit of a blue-eyed inspection worthy of his father.

'Er—then I go to college,' she stated, trying for firmness. 'I worked instead of going to college when I was—was young. Now I intend to go, as soon as term starts in September.'

'Can't imagine why anyone would want to do that,' he muttered. 'They'll only boss you around.'

'Not me!' she said emphatically, and the smile came back into the clear blue eyes and spread across his face.

'No, I expect not; you've got red hair.' He turned his head sideways and contemplated her. 'There used to be a big picture in the house like you. I don't know where it is now.'

'A portrait?' She was very interested. It must have been her father's mother and she would love to see what she had been like.

He nodded. 'I suppose it was. I can just remember it from before I went off to school.' He was looking a little glum and Sophie wanted to put a stop to that quickly.

'Let's search for it,' she suggested enthusiastically, and he was interested at once.

'One day when it's raining,' he agreed. 'We'll go and search the attics when it's raining and dark outside, just like they do in books. Let's shake on it.'

They were just shaking hands seriously, like two conspirators, when Sophie looked up and saw Matthew watching them with a wry expression on his face.

'Tea's up,' he announced, his eyes going from one to the other.

She jumped up, dusting the grass off her jeans, and as Philip skipped ahead Matthew waited to walk beside her.

'What plans were you making?' he enquired quietly.

'None!' She looked up with wide, innocent violet eyes and his glance flashed over her face, his lips once again quirking. He took her arm and she was glad when he looked away and led her off to the café.

'You're going to take some watching, Sophie,' he muttered, almost to himself.

'You have too much to do. Ignore me,' she said quickly.

But his hand tightened slightly on her arm and she could hear the laughter at the back of his voice as he said, 'Believe me, I've tried and failed. I seem to be incapable of ignoring you. When you're there I have to watch you. That's how it is. It must be that fiery hair—moths to the flame.'

'I'm sure I don't know what you mean,' she stated firmly as her legs began to shake slightly but very definitely.

'That,' he assured her sardonically, 'is because you're far too young to understand.' He sighed dramatically. 'Now I have two children on my hands.'

'Oh, do stop it!' she snapped, turning on him with a wild glare, and his hand came to her flushed and angry face, his fingers trailing down her cheek.

'I'm trying, Sophie. You've no idea how hard I'm trying,' he murmured, and she was very glad that they had reached the café and that Philip was waiting impatiently. She was in a complete turmoil; she never had the slightest idea what Matthew was talking about. One thing she did know, though. She was beginning to like it just a little too much when his hand touched her. Maybe she should find a way of going back to London.

But then there was Philip. Without any plan at all she had set her mind on getting him back to his home permanently. There must be good day-schools somewhere close. She had to fix that before she left here.

'You've gone pale, Sophie,' Philip observed, squinting up at her in the sunlight.

'Er—it must be my guilty conscience,' she quipped, and he darted inside for his tea and scones, his grin back in place, but she found herself detained as Matthew's hand fastened into her short, bright curls.

'Is it?' he asked darkly.

'Of course not!' She tried to struggle but gave it up as his fingers tightened.

'Then why the interesting pallor?' He tilted her head back and looked down into her face, searching her expression, and Sophie found her eyes locked with his. They really were the most wonderful eyes—tawny gold, like treasure from the Incas. His dark face too was almost alien, lean and handsome, slightly austere.

'Sophie!' Matthew's sharp admonishment brought her back to the present and her pale cheeks flushed when she realised just how she had been looking at him. He had certainly noticed, too. That was the reason for the sharp tone and he let her go abruptly.

She darted into the comparative darkness of the café but she hadn't reached Philip before Matthew's hand came back to her arm.

'Slow down,' he muttered, and she was glad to hear amusement back in his voice. 'Just remember,' he added, 'that you are constantly bringing on your own attacks of nerves. Don't blame me.'

'I don't.' They were both speaking quickly, as if they had to get things straight before Philip heard, and it made her feel more guilty than ever.

'Are you feeling all right, Sophie?' Matthew asked softly and she nodded, shooting him a quick little smile. If she was not then it was certainly no virus that was making her legs shake. She thought longingly of London but it was no use. There was no money and, in any case, she never gave up on a project—and Philip was a very worthy project.

Over the next few days Sophie found it very easy to get to know Philip, and his presence helped because now she was not alone with Matthew. Dinner was served earlier and Philip stayed up. He was very talkative and, on the surface, happy, but always at the back of his eyes there was a hidden problem.

'Do they call you Philip at school?' she asked one afternoon when they were both in the garden. Matthew was working and Philip was trained not to interrupt when his father's study door was closed.

'The masters do. The boys call me Pip—at least, my friends do. With the bigger boys you just get your other name. They call me Trevelyan.'

Sophie grimaced. How typical! At least, being female, she had never suffered that particular indignity at school. Perhaps the other boys didn't think it an indignity but she could see that Philip was not too happy about it.

'Can I call you Pip?' she asked, and he looked up at her with a smile.

'I wish you would. Dad always says Philip but I'd like to be just Pip. If you call me that he'll say it too.'

Not necessarily, she mused. Names were a bit of a problem in this house. There was her own insistence on being Sophie, Matthew's assertion that she said his full name huskily, and she had never managed to make Biddy call her anything other than Miss Sophie, as if she were a spinster lady of noble birth. Still, perhaps Matthew would learn by example. It remained to be seen.

Esther rang that evening and gave Sophie her splendid news.

'We've decided to get married at the end of the month,' she announced. 'Patrick may have the chance of another job in a hospital further north and it seems stupid to wait. We've got our basic furniture now and we may as well save for the rest when we're married.'

'That's the end of next week!' Sophie was stunned. 'Am I still the bridesmaid?'

'Of course! Your dress is being finished now. I hope you haven't put on too much weight with all those scones. I used the measurements we took before you left.'

'I'll squeeze into it,' Sophie assured her. 'It's getting there that's the problem,' she added anxiously.

It meant getting to London and then finding somewhere to stay. She could always stay with Esther's parents, but they lived a long way out and in any case she hardly knew them.

'What about getting that splendid Matthew to bring you?' Esther asked. 'I'm dying to see him.'

'He's very busy,' Sophie managed quickly. 'He's wrapped up in a new book.'

She couldn't ask Matthew. It would be presuming too much and, anyway, he would refuse. Philip would be back at school by then and she would just have to spend some of her carefully hoarded cash to get to the wedding.

'I'll come by train,' she informed Esther. 'I still have funds.' She did but they were beginning to look very thin indeed and soon she would have to stock up on things like shampoo and make-up. She left the phone in a thoughtful frame of mind and as she was crossing the hall she almost bumped headlong into Matthew.

'What's wrong?' His hand came out to steady her and she shook her head quickly.

'Nothing at all. That was Esther. She's getting married sooner than expected and I'm one of her bridesmaids. I'll have to go to London. The wedding is next weekend.' He just went on looking at her and she felt the inclination to babble. 'Er—my dress is almost ready. We did the measuring before I came down here and——'

'Come into the study,' he ordered quietly. 'There's something I should have done immediately you came down here but with one thing and another it slipped my mind.'

'What?' She hovered at the door as he strode across to his desk.

'Come in. I won't bite you.' He glanced at her and she went forward with very obvious reluctance. This was the holy of holies, the place where he produced the books. Sophie hardly dared to look around. It was the only downstairs room she had not explored. This was Matthew's domain.

He was still watching her, a trifle impatiently.

'Will you kindly stop looking terrified?' he asked testily. 'You make things unnecessarily difficult. I only have to look at you to realise that I'm about to get a short lecture.'

'It all depends on what you want to see me for,' Sophie pointed out stiffly. The shot about her making things difficult had certainly hit home. She knew perfectly well that if she simply went about her business and behaved like a guest she would never clash with Matthew. It was her turbulent character that was to blame.

'I want to see you because I intended to set up a bank account for you the moment you arrived. I forgot about it.'

'I have a bank account, thank you,' she assured him, more stiffly than ever. In no way was she prepared to allow Matthew to give her money. It was bad enough that she had been forced to throw herself on his mercy, and he had shown plenty of that, considering her ways. She would not let him give her anything at all.

'Possibly you have,' he murmured drily. 'Is there any money in it, though?'

'Enough.' She avoided his gaze, and when the silence stretched on muttered, 'It's nice of you to ask...to be concerned but you're not really responsible for me at all, even though—even though you've let me stay here and—and...'

'Have you ever given any thought to being gracious?' he asked coldly. 'You're turning a perfectly straight-forward transaction into a major event. We are both well aware that if you had not been desperate nothing on earth would have got you down here. If you had been at all capable of fending for yourself you would have stayed in London and taken another flat. It doesn't take much to work out that you are therefore short of money. I propose to give you some.'

'No!' She looked across at him firmly. 'You had me here when you didn't need to. I'm nothing more than a stranger—no relative, nothing. I can manage with what I have and——'

'And how do you propose to get to London and stay until the wedding?' he asked in the same cold voice. 'Are you intending to stay with the boyfriend? Or on second thoughts perhaps that's not possible, otherwise you would have stayed there with him instead of coming down here.'

'As a matter of fact he asked me to marry him,' she managed in a defiant voice, and Matthew's dark brows rose sceptically.

'So what went wrong? You thought it was too drastic a measure for tiding you over until September?'

'I've got things to do with my life. I'm going to college and—and getting married is not on the agenda.'

Sophie turned for the door, desperate to escape because she felt as if she had been given a good shaking and for once tears were not very far off. How did one behave graciously in such an embarrassing situation? She wasn't very gracious after all and there was no use denying it. She had always had to fight for herself and that didn't leave much room for genteel behaviour.

CHAPTER SIX

MATTHEW reached her as her hand felt for the handle of the door and his burst of irritation had obviously gone.

'All right, Sophie. I know you're a stubborn, prickly female with iron determination. We'll let the matter of the money go for now.'

'Thank you,' she muttered, still determined to leave speedily. She was thinking of at least three things at once—how to get out graciously, how to face Matthew later and how to manage to get to London without emptying her account.

He took her shoulders and turned her to face him, putting a stop to her flight.

'I'll take you to London. As it happens I have to go up there and we can travel together.'

She looked up at him quickly. If he had to go to London then it was not just some charitable offer. She already knew that Philip was going back to school next Wednesday so Matthew probably did have some business in London. He might be going to see his publisher.

'Well, you've looked for traps and snares, searched for alms-giving,' he murmured as she continued to gaze at him in silence. 'Unless you've found a snag, or intend to travel by rail while I drive to the same city alone, shall we say that I will escort you to London?'

'I'll have to go well before the wedding in case the dress doesn't fit. I'll have to find out what to do too,' Sophie added anxiously.

'No problem. We'll drop Philip off at school and go straight on.'

Wednesday. That should just about do it. There was the worry about where to stay but she could talk that over with Esther.

'Well—well, thank you, then.'

He continued to look down at her, his long fingers moving very slightly on her slender shoulders. She knew he was doing it absent-mindedly but that didn't help much. It was giving her that warm, wobbly feeling again. She dropped her head and stood very still and a shiver ran down her spine at the sound of his low, dark laugh.

'What a weird mixture you are, Sophie,' he murmured softly. 'I'm never quite sure what to do about you.'

'I'll be gone almost before you know it,' she muttered, and for a second his fingers tightened before he let her go and opened the door for her.

'Oh, I'll know it. We'll all know it. I'm not sure whether you're a burst of sunshine or merely a source of constant irritation, but whatever you are you've made quite an impact here. We'll know it when you're out of our lives.'

She made her escape. She was not quite sure what he meant but she assumed that he thought of her as a meddling nuisance. Why couldn't she mind her own business and just get on normally with him? She should just leave well alone. He was still pining for his wife and mixed up with Eve Corwin. There was Philip too. She couldn't let that go by even if it was none of her business.

She sighed and went up the stairs. Her own work was being sadly neglected while she sorted out people who didn't want her help. She would just have to see what happened.

*   *   *

Things happened more quickly than Sophie had anticipated because next day she found Philip looking
thoroughly miserable and, after a good deal of coaxing,
she got the truth out of him. He didn't want to go back
to school.

'Any particular reason?' she asked cautiously. The
desire to tell him that she was not at all surprised was
crushed as she thought of the rage Matthew would be
in if she rushed into this situation feet first.

'I'm not too good at games,' Philip confessed, and at
least she tried to be reasonable.

'Well, lots of people are the same,' she pointed out.
'There are plenty of people who can't do well at games
but usually they manage to shine at something else.'

'I managed that,' he muttered glumly. 'I'm good at
art, and I didn't mind games. I just did my best.'

'So there you are!' she said triumphantly, congratu-
lating herself on being so logical and sober.

'That was before Mr Rowe came,' he confided miserably. 'You can't get out of things with him and he
shouts right across the field.'

Sophie could feel her temper tightening but she stuck
to her attitude. Nobody was going to get the chance to
say that she rushed into this.

'I expect you wouldn't hear him if he didn't. Games
masters blow whistles and shout things. It's the way they
are.'

'He shouts things at *me*,' Philip told her indignantly.
'It makes me feel stupid.'

Thinking rapidly, Sophie could not quite see this as a
valid reason for talking to Matthew about moving his
son closer to home. Everybody had a cross to bear, even
children. It might very well be that the next time Philip
came home he would have turned the vile Mr Rowe into
a hero.

'How long has be been there?' she enquired cautiously.

'Three weeks.'

'Well, he'll probably be trying to show how good he is,' she managed soothingly. 'Give him time, Pip. I expect he'll mellow.'

'Maybe.' Philip sniffed and turned away. 'Let's go down to the beach with my kite.'

She had planned to work but she gave the idea up now. She had the feeling that she had let Pip down. He seemed to have been relying on her. Why he couldn't tell his father these facts she did not know. In all probability Matthew would have said exactly the same sort of things as she had said herself. That made her a pretty hopeless mediator.

The feeling of guilt hung around all evening. Long after dinner was over and Pip had gone to bed Sophie continued to fret over her part in the affair.

It was a wild sort of night. There had been a forecast of rain but for a long time none had come, and then as the darkness had deepened a driving wind had sprung up from the sea, bringing the rain in torrents, lashing it against the windows like steel fingers.

The noise made working hopeless. It was not possible to sit and study with all the turmoil throwing itself at the house. With the thought of Pip being unhappy at the back of her mind, and the gale lashing outside, her mind refused to stay on anything and finally she went downstairs to the sitting-room.

It was quieter there, more sheltered, and now that Biddy had left for home and Pip was asleep the tranquillity of the old house wrapped itself around her. She knew that Matthew would be in his study, working. He had been cooped up in there most days and that hadn't pleased her either. She would have thought that with Pip home he would have spent more time with him, even if he did have a book running wildly in his head.

He had been more available before Pip had come home. Now he was not available at all. She knew why. Pip reminded him of Delphine. He was keeping out of the way. She felt stricken at the thought but Pip was just a little boy. If she had not been here he would have been lonely in the house during his break from school.

He needed a mother. Well, it couldn't be Eve Corwin. *She* was already married and the idea of her being in this house and having anything to do with Pip made Sophie furious. Not that it was anything to do with her. Matthew had called her a ship passing in the night. That thought made her thoroughly miserable too. When she left here she would probably not see Matthew again. Her original plan to leave with a few well-chosen words of thanks was exactly what he would want.

She sighed and turned her face against the soft fabric of the settee. It would have been better never to have come here at all. It had upset her well-planned life. Things would never be the same again because she would always remember Trembath House and Matthew.

Sophie heard a slight noise, and as she looked up she found Matthew standing in the open doorway, watching her.

'Such a heartfelt sigh. You have more problems, Sophie?'

'I told you, I don't really make a habit of having problems,' she pointed out defensively. 'I haven't any at the moment as it happens.'

'You were just practising a sigh for when they came pouring back. I see.' He had that sceptical look on his face again, and his lips were quirking. He often looked at her like that, she mused with annoyance—as if she were some sort of amusing burden. Well, she might be a burden but it was not amusing.

'The person with the problem is Pip,' she stated sharply before she could give herself time to think out the disadvantages of interfering when she had been ordered to mind her own business in no uncertain terms.

'Do I know anyone called Pip?' Matthew looked at her coldly, his amusement quite gone, and she felt her temper begin to rise. He knew exactly whom she was talking about. This was just a further demonstration of his superior manner.

'Philip likes to be called Pip,' she assured him with as much haughtiness as she could summon up. 'We agreed on it. After all, it's *his* name. His friends call him Pip.'

'Splendid,' he remarked caustically, coming right into the room and closing the door with a flick of his hand. It was almost a sinister action and instantly Sophie felt trapped, her courage beginning to ooze silently away. 'So if he has a name he likes, and now counts you friend enough to advise you to use it, what problem does he have?'

It seemed to Sophie that he was coming towards her in a very menacing way—like a big, dark cat silently approaching. There were only two lamps on in the room and they were picking up his amber eyes, making them gleam almost unnaturally.

'Why—why don't you ask him?' she said hurriedly. 'He's your son after all.'

'But I'm asking you, Sophie,' Matthew reminded her silkily. 'I find you sighing away, sitting all by yourself, and naturally I want to know why.'

It wasn't a bit natural to her. Her heart was hammering and she was very glad to be sitting down, even though it meant that he was towering over her.

'He doesn't like school!' she blurted out in a breathless voice. 'He's getting picked on.'

'Bullied?' Matthew's black brows drew together and she shook her head impatiently, annoyed that he didn't know what was in her mind without her having to spell it out to him.

'Not by the boys, no.'

'Then perhaps you had better explain.' He stood watching her, big, dark and on the very edge of temper. Sophie could see it but she had started this and there was no way she was about to back down—not that he would have let her.

'It's a new master—the games master. He seems to think that Pip is some sort of wimp. He roars at him across the games field and makes him feel foolish.'

'Perhaps he has no other way of communicating,' Matthew suggested icily. 'As I recall, games masters roar out orders when they're not blowing whistles.'

'It's not just orders,' she insisted crossly. 'I mean, how can it be? An order doesn't make you feel foolish.'

'What does he say?' Matthew had a very weary look on his face now, as if he were dealing with an idiot, and Sophie got to her feet, ignoring his exceptionally close proximity.

'I don't know what he says! Pip never told me, and I'll tell you why he never told me—because I tried to be reasonable. I remembered your words of warning and I—I fobbed him off with weasel words!' She glared up into his face. 'He was about to tell me why he's so miserable and I let him down. *That's* why I was sighing.'

'Philip is not miserable,' Matthew said forcefully, glowering down at her with more than warning in his eyes now.

'How do you know?' she countered. 'You sit in that study and never come out. Pip is miserable about going back to school.'

'Leave it!' he ordered sharply. 'This is none of your affair.' He turned to leave but by now Sophie was beside herself with annoyance. He was so damned superior and he hadn't paid any attention at all to what she had said.

'All right, I'll leave it,' she raged, 'but don't blame me if you're building up trouble for later. Don't blame me that you're losing track of what Pip needs. If you two had been close he would have told you his problems but he told me instead and I'm just a stranger. I know what miserable is!'

'Not as much as you're going to know if you keep on like this,' Matthew threatened, turning his head to frown at her fiercely.

'I don't care,' she informed him furiously. 'You'll be the one who loses when Pip goes all introverted and peculiar. You can't even see it coming. You're thick as a stick!'

He turned back to her then with a movement so violent that had she been in her right senses she would have run. She was not in her right senses, however, and when he rasped out, 'Shut up, Sophie!' she was so frustrated that she pushed at his powerful chest with both hands.

'Don't push me!'

He grasped her shoulders with hands like steel. His fingers bit into her through the soft wool of her sweater and she saw violence in the amber blaze of his eyes. He pulled her relentlessly closer, his grip too tight for any struggle on her part, and all she could do was try to glare back. 'So I'm thick as a stick?' he growled menacingly. 'I must be to have you in the house.'

'I'll go!' she snapped, wriggling her shoulders to free herself from his tightening grip.

'Oh, no, you won't. You'll stay and behave yourself. I think you've just shown that Pip needs you. What you will do, though, Sophrina, is become much more tame.'

Sophie opened her mouth to rage about this use of her hated name but no words ever escaped her parted lips. Matthew swooped on her with the same menace that he had shown when he had first walked into the

room, with the same menace that had been in his eyes
for the past few minutes, if only she had not been too
enraged to see it.

His mouth covered hers harshly, giving her no way of
escaping, and a wave of sheer panic hit her as she felt
the hardness of the male body pressed close to her own.
It was wrong, her mind told her. Matthew had nothing
to do with her at all and he certainly did not have the
right to chastise her so brutally. She froze inside, unable
to take any action at all.

Even through her numbing panic her instincts sur-
vived and she felt that he despised himself for this
ruthless punishment. It went on, though, all the same,
until Sophie went limp in his arms. It was not the first
time that she had been kissed, but she had never been
kissed in so adult a manner, had never been so aware of
the hard proximity of a male body.

When Andy kissed her it was almost amusing and they
usually ended up spluttering with laughter. There was
nothing amusing about Matthew's kiss. It was not really
a kiss at all, she reminded herself. It was an angry punishment. But all the same she was aware of him as she
had never before been aware of anyone.

For a second more he held her fast, his hard arms
supporting her slender, trembling body. His lips moved
briefly over hers, tentatively, exploringly, and then, with
a low growl of annoyance, he held her away, seemingly
aware that if he simply let her go she would sink to the
floor.

When she looked up, almost fearfully, he was staring
into her eyes, and even as she watched his gaze hardened
over. She took a long, shuddering breath and he let her
go then.

'Don't expect an apology,' he grated as her violet eyes
got bigger and bigger. 'You've interfered where you have
no right to, taken me to task verbally and even had the

temerity to push me. Just understand that you're staying here for a little while and then you'll be gone. You have your plans, Sophie, and I have mine. You seem to be getting on well with Philip and maybe you'll even write to him when you leave us but you will not in any way change his life or mine. Remember that!'

For a minute she stared at him, shaken and hurt. Where the hurt was coming from she didn't know but it was there all the same. It was monstrous that he thought that he could treat her like this and ridiculous that it mattered.

'You've told me before,' she managed bleakly. 'Ships that pass in the night. Well, it won't be for long. This ship will be steaming over the horizon before you even know it.'

She turned and walked out, hoping that he didn't know how her legs were shaking, and he said nothing at all, even when she slammed the door behind her. She ran up to her room and stared at herself in the mirror, quite startled that she didn't feel at all like crying, and equally surprised that the well-known rage did not surface.

She was shocked, that was it. Nobody had treated her like that before. She nodded at her reflection. It explained the unusual feelings that raced through her, the way her mind tended to dwell on the feel of Matthew's body against her own, and the sensations that had surged through her at the last minute when his lips had made a lightning exploration of her mouth.

Sophie turned away in disgust. She must be quite mad, trying to make something of a fierce and chauvinistic chastisement. She had to get away from here.

The glimmerings of an idea surfaced. At the wedding she would hint a little and see what happened. If she could just get somewhere to stay temporarily she might be able to get some sort of job to see her through until September. After all, she was not ill now; that hurdle had been passed. Now her problems were simply accommodation and a little cash.

Her mind dwelt for a moment on the money left to her by her parents. Would it be released for this emergency? She had always sworn never to touch it, but her childish hurt had passed now and deep inside she knew that if she didn't watch her wayward emotions she would be heading for a much more serious hurt.

The rain was still lashing against the windows and the roar of the sea was almost frightening. Not quite, though. She stood at the window. It was too dark to see anything but the same old excitement swirled over her at the wild and angry sound of the waves. She might have been born to live in this windswept house. How had her grandmother felt about it? Had she too had this love for the untamed elements, the majestic sound of an unconquered sea?

Sophie grimaced and got ready for bed. Her grandmother had been unhappy and she would do well to remember that. Maybe Matthew was as cruel and unfeeling as his father had been? She shook her head. No, he was not. His eyes and his lips smiled much too much for cruelty to be rooted in his nature. He still missed his wife. That simple fact explained everything.

It was her too. She and Matthew were incompatible and her constant probing into his affairs simply made it worse. As soon as she had come here she had walked straight into trouble with her enquiry about Delphine. She supposed he would never really forgive her for that. It must have been a shock to him.

She went to sleep making plans that merely increased her misery because deep down she knew perfectly well that she did not want to leave Trembath House. It had got into her blood and so had Matthew Trevelyan.

*   *   *

The following day the bad weather continued and this time it did not please Sophie. She had been hoping to get out of the house today—maybe walk down to the village—and ask Pip if he wanted to accompany her. She was at great pains to avoid Matthew but, as it turned out, he was not at breakfast and, considering the state of the weather, she assumed that he had abandoned his usual swim and had eaten earlier.

It might have been, of course, that he was avoiding her too, but it seemed unlikely. It was more in his character to sit and glower at her for the previous day's crimes. He certainly would not have considered that his behaviour was in any way bad.

Whatever the reasons, she felt restless and still miserable—too restless to settle in her room with her books. She did, though, because she wished to keep out of Matthew's way, but the grey, weeping sky and the mournful sound of the sea constantly intruded on her studies.

She was glad when, in the early part of the afternoon, Pip knocked on her door and stuck his head inside. At least he looked cheerful and she smiled back at him as she invited him to come in.

'What about today, Sophie?' he prompted eagerly. 'Remember we said we would search the attic for that big picture on a rainy day?'

'Oh, yes!' She tried to sound enthusiastic but the thought of going up there and poking about without Matthew's permission made her quake a little. She was not about to find him and ask his permission either. 'Do you think you should ask your father first?' she ventured, but Pip looked at her with pitying eyes.

'Sophie! I live here. I can do exactly as I like unless it's dangerous. Dad told me that *years* ago!' he finished expansively, and in the face of this kindly disdain Sophie had no choice other than to agree. All the same she was looking over her shoulder a good deal as they climbed to the next floor where there were three unused bedrooms, and she was not at all settled in her mind until Pip pointed to a door and announced that that one led to the attic steps.

There were plenty of lights but on such a dark and gloomy day they seemed to be inadequate, and Sophie was glad when they at last stepped into a long room that seemed to stretch over the whole top of the house. There were only two overhead lights there, both naked bulbs, and, far from being exciting, it was decidedly spooky.

Pip, though, was filled with zest for the search and began at once to dive into boxes and chests that seemed to have been untouched for generations.

'There's some funny stuff here, Sophie!' he called out eagerly. 'Look at this!' He held up an old brass telescope. 'It might have belonged to a pirate or a smuggler. Do you think smugglers once lived in Trembath House?'

'Unlikely,' she muttered uneasily. 'Too grand for the likes of them. Let's find the portrait and go.' She had visions of Matthew storming in and telling her off for allowing this excursion, and actually it was extremely eerie up there. There were sombre shadows in the corners of the huge room and her vivid imagination could see Trevelyans from way back, all glaring at her, all with dark faces like Matthew's and gleaming golden eyes.

'Scaredy cat!' Pip shrieked gleefully as he saw her face, and that put her on her mettle.

'Certainly not! It's just that I have things to do. Now let's find that portrait.'

It was not long, however, before Pip's inquisitive nature fired her with enthusiasm too, and the search for her grandmother's portrait was forgotten as they rummaged through the old chests and boxes, poring over their finds like treasure hunters. There were things stored that had been untouched for many, many years and Sophie was fascinated.

Pip climbed on a box to use the telescope and view the pounding sea from the sloping window but Sophie hardly noticed. She had found an old wooden rack and in it were stacked many pictures. They were carefully covered but their shape and size told her exactly what they were and she began to unwrap them silently.

Mostly they were old oil-paintings and for all she knew they might have been valuable but the only thing that made her heart beat rapidly was one that had been placed almost in the middle of the others. As soon as she saw the edge of the gilt frame she knew what it would be, and with great care she unwrapped the thing that she had come up here to find.

The woman was beautiful. There was the same brilliant colouring—the violet eyes and glittering red hair. Whoever had painted her had done so before she'd become sad and ill, because she was smiling, obviously full of life and happiness.

The artist had known her ways, too, because he had not placed her in some indoor setting. Wherever she had been to pose for the picture the artist had finally given her a background of sea and sky, the wild Cornish waves breaking on a sandy shore without the fury that Sophie had come to expect.

It was wonderful, touching, and in spite of the fact that she had never known her father's mother Matthew's words had sunk deep into her mind and tears came to her eyes.

'Margaret.' The voice made her jump and she looked round to see Matthew standing behind her, looking down at the vivid likeness of the woman he had adored. 'Margaret Grant who became Margaret Trevelyan.'

'She was beautiful,' Sophie whispered, almost afraid to speak in case he cast off the reminiscent look and concentrated on her and her latest transgression.

'Like you,' he agreed quietly. 'I don't know how Quentin could bear to have you out of his sight, let alone pack you off to school and never see you. He loved his mother.'

'People do things for—for strange reasons,' she ventured, glancing up at him. He should understand if anyone did. Maybe her father had let her go because she'd reminded him painfully of his mother, but Matthew should know all about that. Didn't he let Pip go so far away because he reminded him of Delphine? If she was like her grandmother, how much was Pip like Delphine? There didn't seem to be anything of Matthew in him. His astonishing fairness, his blue eyes were not in any way even touched by the Trevelyan darkness.

'I suppose they do,' Matthew said harshly. For a moment he seemed to be glaring down at her and then, as she continued to look uneasy, he suddenly smiled. 'Don't look as if you're about to flee, Sophie,' he coaxed softly. 'I've recovered from my burst of temper. Last night was not exactly typical of me. Male chauvinism is not one of my traits, although I agree I can be something of a brute.'

'I—I've quite forgotten last night,' she lied anxiously. 'If I'm looking uneasy it's because I wondered if Pip is allowed up here.'

They both glanced across to where Pip stood gazing out at the wet and stormy day, his eye glued to the old telescope.

'Why not?' Matthew murmured. 'This place is great fun on a gloomy day. Quentin and I spent hours up here. If you root about long enough you'll find some of our old things.'

'No, thank you,' she said quickly. 'I only agreed to come up to look for this. Pip said he might have seen it. He—he said there was a picture that looked like me and I thought it might be here as you had already told me that she—that I...'

'That you reminded me of your beautiful grandmother,' he finished for her. 'Now that you've found it, what do you intend to do?'

'Nothing. I have work to do and I should be getting on with it. If I'm not careful September will creep up on me and I won't be ready.'

'Then don't let me stop you.' The smile left his eyes and his voice sounded harsh suddenly, and Sophie didn't quite know what to do.

'I can't really leave Pip,' she began. 'It's a long way up here and——'

'You're not his nursemaid,' Matthew grated. 'Pip spends plenty of wet days up here. He's more than capable of taking care of himself, in spite of your thoughts to the contrary.'

He turned away and went across to his son and Sophie looked frustratedly at his back. He certainly knew how to crush her. Now she felt utterly left out of things. She went down the stairs to her own floor and shut herself in for the rest of the day. Let him spend his valuable hours with Pip. It was about time anyway.

At dinner Matthew was coolly polite and it was a very uneasy meal as far as Sophie was concerned. The fact that Pip was there seemed to make it even more awkward, and every time she looked up Matthew seemed to be regarding her with sombre, thoughtful eyes. He was probably wondering how he could get rid of her gracefully.

She was glad when he went out to his study but she felt too uneasy to work. She watched television with Pip, but he was accustomed to early nights and at eight-thirty he went off to bed. So Sophie sat alone, until the storm upset the transmitter and she was left staring at a blank screen. It seemed to be a signal to go to bed too.

The moment she walked into her room she knew that something was different. She stood at the door and looked round but it was only as she walked in and looked at the wall behind the door, the stretch of wall that led to her bathroom, that she stopped and gasped. The portrait of her grandmother was hanging there, facing her bed, and only Matthew could have put it there.

It had been dusted and carefully mounted on the wall and her heart gave a great leap of joy at this kindness. She was still gazing at it with glowing eyes when Matthew came and leaned against the open door, a half-smile on his face.

'Does it please the Lady Sophrina?' he asked in a low voice, and she turned to him with a smile that lit up her whole face.

'Oh, yes! Can I keep it here until I go?' she asked breathlessly.

'You can keep it always, Sophie,' he told her quietly. 'If it belongs to anyone at all it belongs to you.'

'But—but it's a family portrait; I mean...'

'Surely you've noticed that I don't go in for family portraits?' he questioned, stepping into the room and looking up at the likeness of her grandmother. 'Even if I did, Margaret was not really my family. I only wished it. She belonged to Quentin and now to you.'

'I'm sorry,' she murmured, turning away. 'I'm sorry she didn't stay long enough to make things different.'

'Nothing would have made things different,' he said sombrely. He suddenly turned her to face him and looked down at her. 'You, my fiery little Sophie, have brought a spark of life to Trembath but you will go too, like a boat that comes into harbour and then leaves for some unknown port. Nothing makes any difference.'

'I understand how you feel . . .' she began, but he suddenly grinned at her and raised her chin lightly.

'I doubt it. Whatever is going on in your agile mind it is almost certain to be a creation of your fertile imagination. Don't——'

'Interfere?' she interrupted, and he laughed even more.

'I was about to say don't worry your glowing head about the Trevelyans. We're a hard breed.'

'Is Pip?' she asked before she could stop herself, and for a moment the amber eyes narrowed.

'Time will tell,' he said softly. 'Go to bed, Sophie, and gaze at your grandmother. Remind yourself that her life would have been very different if she had not come to Cornwall. Glowing creatures like that and Black Cornish do not, and never will, mix.'

When he had gone Sophie sat for a long time and looked at the portrait. Matthew had given it to her and she would keep it. It had given her a past when she had always felt slightly lost. Matthew had given her a past too, and she could not imagine readily giving up the present with him.

It would have to be done, though. He had made it very plain that he expected her to go when the time came, and he had hinted that he would not want to see her again. The kiss had just been his way of calling her to order. All the same, it hadn't left her mind since it had happened. In some mysterious way it had changed her.

CHAPTER SEVEN

PIP was driven back to school on Wednesday. Sophie took enough clothes for three days. As Matthew was almost certainly coming back the next day after he had completed whatever business was taking him to London, she would have to make her own way back here.

On the surface Pip seemed to be cheerful, although he did not leave for school with a great deal of delight, and when he got out of the car on their arrival he came round to speak to Sophie while his father was unloading the luggage.

'Are you making a plan, Sophie?' he whispered, his head stuck through the open window of the car.

'About what?' She was startled. She usually was making some plan or other, but lately she had put such things to the very back of her mind as they had brought her a good deal of trouble.

'About school!' he hissed. 'I was sure you would get Dad to move me.' He looked very let-down and she bit at her lip thoughtfully.

'Do you really want to leave this place?' she asked. 'It looks good to me.' It was astonishing what treachery she was prepared to practise for Matthew's sake. It had not looked anything like good when she had first seen it, and as far as she could tell the half-term had not improved it. It would not have improved a heartless games master either.

'I can stick it if I have to,' he said stiffly, and that put an end to her wavering. She gave his arm a squeeze and leaned over to kiss his cheek.

113

'Leave it with me,' she murmured in his ear. 'Big plan coming up.'

'Oh, great, Sophie!' He was smiling widely as Matthew came round to collect him, and they both received a rather suspicious glance from the amber eyes.

'What was all that about?' Matthew enquired as they finally pulled away. 'You've been making some arrangement with Philip?'

'Er—no,' she assured him uneasily. 'It was just that— well, I'll be here when he comes home for Easter. He's glad.'

'Naturally.' Matthew shot her a sceptical look and pulled out into the main road that went past the school. He said nothing more about the incident except to murmur almost to himself, 'For someone who has so many woes you certainly like to live dangerously, Lady Sophrina.'

'Why are you calling me that when we have an understanding?' she asked a trifle sharply and he shrugged.

'It seems to pop into my head; you really must forgive me. It's being a writer. I have this romantic imagination. I often see you as a lady of long ago—bright hair, flowing robes and glowing violet eyes. There really must be a book there somewhere.'

Sophie kept quiet. The idea was not at all unpleasant, and when Matthew said her hated name like that it didn't seem to be bad at all—Lady Sophrina in flowing robes against a backdrop of stormy seas. The scene was impossible to imagine without the house coming into it. Take her away from there and she was just plain Sophie. Take her away from there and she was a person with no past or future.

She grunted irritably. At this rate she would be begging to stay forever and it was just not like her. She glanced secretly at Matthew and she was not at all surprised to see those lips quirking again. He always knew exactly what he was doing. He never said anything without some ulterior motive.

She settled down for the long drive and tried hard to think what he could be up to with his romantic and historical thoughts. There was definitely no book in it for him. His books were best-sellers of the terrifying variety. They did not lean to romance and neither did Matthew Trevelyan. He was all hard, dark intelligence—too much for her probably, but she would have to see. She had now made a promise of sorts to Pip.

Sophie sighed to herself. More problems and this time not even her own. First things first. She had this wedding to attend, and the worry of where to stay loomed up, cutting off any further wandering speculation and making her silent for much of the way.

She was not at all pleased to see London. She had forgotten how busy it was, how much traffic there was and how people hurried along enveloped in their own personal clouds. Now that they had arrived she didn't know what to say to Matthew. At any moment he was going to ask where he should drop her off and, apart from mentioning the hospital where Esther worked, she couldn't think of anywhere.

He asked her nothing at all and she sat like a mouse when finally he pulled up outside a quiet terrace of comfortable-looking houses in a Kensington street.

'Where is this?' she asked anxiously, and Matthew got out and opened the door for her, quite obviously determined that she should get out too.

'My London pad,' he told her sardonically. 'When Philip is at school and the sound of the sea gets on my nerves I sneak off here.'

'Oh, I see!' she muttered, and his next words quite took her breath away.

'We'll stay here while we're in London. This way I can keep an eye on you.'

'I'm twenty-two going on twenty-three,' she reminded him sternly. 'I've been keeping an eye on myself for years.'

'And very well too,' he soothed sarcastically, 'until the sky fell on you in the form of a demolished house, redundancy and a virus. We'll take no chances. You're with me now.'

Sophie was not at all sure how to take this, but it got her out of a tricky situation for the time being and she allowed him to lead her into the quiet of the house. There was no traffic noise here, and although for the past few miles she had been mulling over the fact that she no longer liked traffic its absence now alarmed her.

'There's no noise,' she said quickly, but Matthew was evidently in one of his taunting moods.

'Give me a few minutes,' he drawled, 'and I'll create a level of noise to set your mind at rest.'

'I didn't mean . . .' she began, feeling her cheeks begin to burn, and he turned to her with amused eyes.

'I've worked out all by myself that you have nowhere to stay. This is a place to stay. There is no ulterior motive, except to keep you safe. We work out a timetable. I either take you where you wish to go or I put you in a taxi. You get ready for the wedding, you attend the wedding and I deal with my business meetings. After that we go back together. No problem.'

On the face of it the idea sounded very good but still Sophie was uneasy.

'You don't need to do things for me . . .' she began, and he quirked an eyebrow at her as he made for the front door.

'Left to yourself you might just start organising other people's affairs,' he pointed out drily. 'I would have to pick up the pieces. This way is easier because I keep control. I'll get the luggage.'

Settled in her room, Sophie mused that it was a good idea after all. Also, Matthew was taking her back with him. That was a pleasing thought. She felt quite light-hearted, and after they had been out for an evening meal she settled in happily and put her clothes into the wardrobe.

Being happy was a bit tricky, she decided after a while, because there was no way she could settle to sleep. For one thing she was missing the constant sound of the sea, and for another she was extremely aware that Matthew was in the small house with her. Somehow it was different from being at Trembath—more intimate—and finally she decided that a cup of tea was absolutely essential. She put on her dressing-gown and went to find the kitchen.

Matthew had made no attempt to go to bed even though he had driven so far, and when she peeped into the sitting-room he was reading.

'Can I make myself a cup of tea?' she asked as he glanced up.

'Of course. Make one for me.'

'How do you like it?' she questioned and he just went on reading.

'Hot and wet.' That was annoying. He was back to the usual taunting and she looked at him severely.

'I'll need a little more information than that.'

'It's about time you knew what I like,' he remarked obscurely. 'We'll start with the tea. One lesson is all you get. I like it very hot, medium-strong, a little milk and sweet—two sugars.'

'Isn't that bad for your teeth?' she muttered thoughtlessly, and he looked across at her then, his white teeth gleaming as he laughed. She fled to the kitchen and made a great deal of fuss about the kettle and the teacups. Why was she always saying things like that? He probably thought she was mad. She wasn't too sure about that herself.

When she carried the tea in he was still reading and she had trouble handing him his cup. For some reason her hand was shaking, and he reached forward and took the cup deftly from her, placing it on the table by his side.

'There,' he announced. 'I managed to get it without being scalded.'

'I wouldn't have dropped it on you,' Sophie protested, and he shot her a wry glance.

'I wasn't about to take the chance.' He moved along the settee. 'Sit down, Tiger Lily, and tell me about this wedding.'

'Why are you calling me that?' She perched on the settee with her tea and felt very wary. Matthew seemed to be in an odd, light-hearted mood and she wasn't sure what that meant.

'Your colouring.' He gave a very theatrical sigh. 'I suppose I'm teasing you again. Try very hard to forgive me. Now tell me about this wedding. I know nothing at all about your friends.'

No, Sophie mused. They had done more arguing than chatting about her life. Tonight was different, though. She felt different and Matthew was being quite gentle. It was nice being close to him. She wriggled to get more comfortable, letting the warm feeling flow through her as she started to tell him about Esther and Patrick and their plans. It took a while and he listened very carefully, putting in the odd question that let her know he was interested.

'And what about the boyfriend?' he asked unexpectedly. 'What's his name? Andrew? Is he going to be there?'

'Oh, yes,' Sophie assured him. 'I certainly hope so. I don't know many people who will be there. I'll need Andy's support.'

'You feel in need of support?' When she turned back from putting her cup down Matthew was watching her with narrowed eyes and she nibbled at her lip.

'Not usually, but lately...'

'I'll be there to collect you,' he assured her, and she looked into his eyes with more eagerness than she realised.

'Would you like to come? I mean I can easily ask Esther and she would just love to meet the famous Matthew Trevelyan.'

'Thank you, no,' he murmured wryly. 'I can manage to fill my time.'

'I was trying to be friendly,' she muttered, beginning to get up. She should have known that Matthew would not want to go. He wouldn't know anyone except her and he had probably seen enough of her as it was.

'And I was trying not to be involved,' he murmured. He took her arm and pulled her back to her seat. 'Don't run off. I thought we were both comfortable. I suppose I've hurt your feelings again?'

'No. It doesn't matter.' She looked down at her toes. Her dressing-gown had ridden up over her ankles and she was not wearing anything on her feet. 'And if you're thinking I was trying to organise you—I wasn't.'

'We seem to be constantly organising each other,' he muttered. 'The fact is, Sophie, I don't want to be drawn any further into your life. I've been in someone's life before.'

The sharp burst of dismay that those words brought was squashed as she realised he meant that he had been hurt when Delphine died.

'It's not the same, though, is it?' she said quickly. 'I know you're still miserable about... This was only a friendly gesture.'

'Maybe I don't feel friendly,' he suggested quietly. He gave her a quizzical look. 'Maybe I would give Andrew a good shaking. I don't suppose he's old enough to be given a sound beating.'

She looked at him in bewilderment. Actually she had no idea what he was talking about, but her heart was thumping alarmingly and she realised once again that she was no match for this dark and unusual man.

He glanced down at her feet and a slow smile tilted his lips.

'You have very pretty toes,' he told her softly. 'What a good job you're not going to the wedding in bare feet. Nobody would even glance at the bride and I would be furious.'

Sophie made an odd little sound in her throat. It was a mixture of fear and excitement and the amber eyes darkened as he looked into the wide violet of her gaze.

'Flowing robes, glowing eyes and fiery hair. You're dressed for the part tonight, Lady Sophrina. All you need is Trembath and the sound of the sea.'

She couldn't speak or move, and when he collected her she came so willingly and softly that his breath rasped in his throat and the narrowed eyes flared with golden light. He held her against him and looked down into her face.

'I'm dangerous, Sophie,' he murmured darkly. 'Just as dangerous as you imagined. Don't come so willingly.'

Still she didn't speak. All she could do was gaze back into his eyes. They seemed to be so compelling, the deep gold edged with thick black lashes, and Sophie was almost saddened that she hadn't noticed that before— as if she had wilfully missed something about him. In her mind the dark outline of Trembath seemed to wrap

itself around them, the surging sound of the sea filling
her head as his hand cupped her face.

'How you pry into my mind, Sophie,' he said softly.
'Into my affairs and into my mind—wondering,
searching, never leaving well alone. Have you wondered
about this?' Before she could even begin to think his
dark head bent and the lips that had punished her so
harshly the other night closed firmly over her own.

She didn't struggle. She admitted to herself dreamily
that she had often wondered about how it would be if
Matthew kissed her properly. The thought that he must
kiss Eve had frequently come into her head and the idea
had made her miserable. She was not miserable now,
though. It was perfect.

There was no inclination to laugh as she did when
Andrew kissed her because this was so different. If she
let go the whole world would disappear and she would
float off into a dream of pleasure and excitement. His
lips probed hers enquiringly and Sophie sighed with
rapture, her mouth opening to the unspoken command.
Whatever Matthew ordered she would do. Obeying
seemed to be so natural.

Her whole body softened against him and he gathered
her closer with a fierce movement that seemed to enclose
her in the masculine hardness of his being. His hand
cupped her head, his fingers tightening in the fiery curls
as he tilted her face, and her arms stole softly around
his neck. For a few moments he seemed willing to be
lost in the waves too. His hand stroked down her back,
arching her closer, enjoying the soft feel of her body,
and then, abruptly, he turned his face away.

He was still holding her tightly, his breathing erratic,
and she could not even begin to think of moving her
arms from his neck.

'I'm years older than you, Sophie,' he said unevenly
against her face. 'I don't suppose you even knew that

every time I see you I want to do that. I'm supposed to be looking after you.' He drew back, carefully dislodging her arms and moving away from her. 'My God! I expected a sort of child when I invited you to Cornwall. I must have been out of my mind.'

It hurt her badly. She was still dreamy, flushed and lost, and she knew that she had to get out of the room fast. She got shakily to her feet.

'I never asked to be invited,' she managed huskily. 'I never asked you to—to kiss me either.'

Matthew looked up at her derisively.

'It depends on what you mean by "asked",' he told her drily. 'Your very presence is enough. Just one glance at you is enough to make any man want to gather you up. Still, I suppose it's not the first time. I expect you react as sweetly when Andrew kisses you.'

Sophie walked to the door, making her exit as fast as possible, but she couldn't let that go. It was almost an insult.

'Yes, Andrew kisses me,' she answered bitterly. 'As to the reaction, though, I usually giggle. I can't seem to help it.'

'Sophie!' The wry mockery died on his face and he half rose from his seat but she had had enough. She didn't want an apology, and she didn't want to be told that she had asked for it without words even if she had. She turned away and walked through the door.

'Goodnight,' she said sharply as she closed it behind her. She was just able to hear Matthew swear under his breath as he dropped back to the settee. It gave her some small amount of satisfaction. At least he would be feeling guilty. What she was feeling she could not describe. She had never felt it before.

She raced to her bed and pulled the covers over her head. But it was a long time before she went to sleep. There was too much excitement, too much longing. Now she knew why she had felt that she would never forget Matthew Trevelyan and it was all so very hopeless. To him it had been simply an interesting experiment that had backfired.

It had changed things too. Now she would not be able to go back with him. She would have to go back to the original plan of dropping hints for help. Surely there would be somebody in Esther's circle who would give her a room for the remaining months? Her mind went back to the solicitor. She would go to see him and ask if there was some way around the will. Maybe she hadn't listened properly before. The money had been for university and that was exactly where she was going.

If she stayed with Matthew she knew that she would end up lost and unhappy. He had come to mean too much to her in such a short time and there was a long time to go to September.

Sophie was surprised to find that she had slept well and much more than surprised when Matthew awakened her by bringing her a cup of tea. He was very quiet and she felt quite flustered when he stood looking down at her.

'What time is it?' she managed at last, and he glanced at his watch.

'It's eight. I have an appointment at ten but I can take you wherever you want to go first.'

She struggled up in bed, avoiding his eyes. 'I can't see Esther until lunchtime,' she told him, 'but I want to go somewhere else. I could take a taxi, though.'

'Whatever you want,' he said coldly. 'If you want to see the boyfriend before lunchtime he could call here.'

'I have no idea what Andrew is doing today,' she informed him sharply as the memory of last night flooded back and with it her hurt. 'I have somewhere to go, as I said.'

'All right. I'll take you or call you a taxi.' She just nodded, and he hesitated before saying, 'Sophie, about last night——'

'I don't want to talk about it, please,' she told him stiffly. 'It was obviously all a silly mistake. During the day I'll forget about it. Once I'm with my friends——'

'No doubt!' He turned and walked out, and for once she had the uncanny feeling that she had won that round. She didn't exactly know how but it felt like that. Not that it gave her much satisfaction. There was no way that she would forget—not today and probably not ever. It would not do, though, for Matthew to know that.

She hurried to get up and make breakfast although she didn't feel like eating. Neither did Matthew, apparently, because she could see that he was only eating to be polite. Later she insisted on getting a taxi because she did not want Matthew to know that she was about to try her hand at forcing her money from the solicitor.

In the event, it proved to be very little problem.

'If you had mentioned all this to me earlier,' Mr Brown pointed out, with a severe look, 'I could have saved you the unnecessary hardship of going down to Cornwall. The money is for your education. Now that you intend to go to university and have all the papers to prove it I really can't see how it could be withheld. The bank, of course, is the executor. This afternoon I will contact them and see what can be worked out. It may take some time but I'll telephone you at—where is it—Trembath House? I believe I still have the number from the time when——'

'No!' Sophie said hastily. 'I'll get in touch with you.'

Even as she was speaking she knew exactly why she was doing this. It had been no hardship to go to Cornwall but it had changed her life completely in so many ways. In spite of her plans to leave Matthew she would be taking away her only excuse to stay with him if she suddenly had money. Of course, she would have to go eventually. After last night staying at Trembath would be impossible, but the thought of going back now and telling him that she might soon have funds and would not need to stay with him was horrifying.

In the first place it would be so ungrateful, and in the second place she would never see him again after that. The thought of it was enough to make her behave very circumspectly.

'I really have no time to give you an appointment for quite a while,' Mr Brown stated rather pompously, and Sophie dug her heels in.

'Then I'll phone you,' she insisted. 'Some time next week. If you can't answer the phone leave me a message.'

She could see from his expression as she left that he found her no more reasonable than he had when she had stormed out of his office so long ago, and once out on the street she really began to wonder if she had done the right thing. Of course she had! There was little point in clinging to Matthew, however strong her inclination. Going away soon was the very best thing to do.

When she met Esther the day took on a certain amount of speed because she was swept away to try on her dress, and after so long apart the words flew thick and fast. Esther wanted to know all about Cornwall, all about Matthew Trevelyan, and when Sophie told her that he had brought her to London and would be taking her back, that she was staying at his London house, Esther gave her what could only be described as an old-fashioned look.

'Is romance in the air?' she asked, with deep interest, and Sophie found her cheeks flushing painfully.

'Don't be ridiculous, Esther! Matthew is—is years older than me.'

'How old?' she persisted.

'As far as I can make out he's thirty-four.' Sophie tried to sound offhand but Esther had great persistence when she was interested.

'Thirty-four? Goodness, girl, that's nothing! Why, you're nearly twenty-three yourself.'

'Well, Matthew says he's a good deal older than me,' Sophie muttered unthinkingly, and Esther's gaze sharpened at once.

'Ah!' Seeing Sophie's distress, she said nothing else, but Sophie was left with the decided impression that in some way she had told her friend much too much. Not that there was anything to tell, she reminded herself. Matthew had kissed her—twice—and she had drifted off on to a pink cloud. Probably everyone he kissed drifted off. She should be grateful that she was her father's daughter and that Matthew had not taken things any further.

'We'll meet Patrick and Andrew and go out for a meal this evening,' Esther stated after a long look at Sophie's gloomy face. At least it meant that she would not be at the mercy of Matthew's black moods. It might even bring her to her senses. Sophie agreed heartily.

It was late as Andrew, Patrick and Esther took her back to Kensington, and it was only then that Sophie realised that she did not have a key to the house. She mentioned this worrying thought to Esther but Patrick was not at all put out.

'No problem,' he assured her. 'If this important person is out you can come back and stay at my place. There's a spare room,' he added with a grin as both Esther and Sophie turned on him with outraged eyes. It meant that there was some rather loud laughter as Sophie got out of the car, and she knew that it was safe to wave them off because Matthew was certainly at home—the lights were all on.

He opened the door just as the car was pulling away and she could see that this time he was a lot more than gloomy. He was furious. He let her know in no uncertain manner as she stepped into the hall.

'Where the hell have you been?' he grated, standing and glaring at her. 'You've been out all day and I had no idea where to start looking for you!'

Sophie was dumbfounded. She had never given a moment's thought to the fact that she was in any way answerable to Matthew. Before she had met him she had spent many years making sure that she was answerable to no one at all. Even so, she found herself explaining away her conduct.

'I told you I had to try my dress on for the wedding,' she reminded him. 'I also had somewhere else to go.'

'It took all day to try on a dress and make this mysterious visit?' he rasped. 'What did you do about eating? How did you get from place to place? Why didn't you get in touch with me?'

She straightened up and faced him. This was no good. She had to let him know that she would do exactly as she liked and she wondered how he would take it when she finally told him about her visit to the solicitor. Maybe it would be better not to tell him at all.

'I've spent most of the day with Esther,' she informed him quietly. 'This evening Esther, Patrick, Andrew and I went for a meal. They dropped me off on the way from there.'

'So I heard!' he snapped. 'I doubt very much if anyone in that car was fit to drive.' He took a step closer, grasping her arm when she automatically backed off. '*I* am looking after you, Miss Grant, and I can do without wasting my day worrying about you. In future you'll tell me exactly where you're going and for how long!'

'I will not!' Sophie's eyes began to flash purple sparks. 'It took me a long time to get rid of authority and I'm not about to be dictated to now. Today is Thursday. Tomorrow I have to be out most of the day with Esther, doing things for the wedding. She gets married on Saturday afternoon and that's that. If you imagine that I'm going to spend tomorrow ringing you up and accounting for myself you're mistaken!'

Matthew glared at her and when she tried to release her arm from his grasp he merely tightened his hold. She began to think that he intended to stand in the hall all night and make her stay there too, but he suddenly relaxed.

'All right. I suppose after being cooped up at Trembath you were bound to want some freedom.'

He was speaking to her as if she were some sort of wayward child, and as Sophie was still annoyed she snapped back at him immediately.

'I'm neither a teenager nor a caged animal,' she flared. 'I don't have to be let out for a run. I had things to do, *business* to attend to!' She jerked her arm free and moved to go to her room. 'And as to being cooped up at Trembath House—I love it there. It has as much freedom as I need.' She spun round and glared at him. 'Houses don't trap you, *people* trap you—people who think they can dictate.'

'People like me,' he concluded, scowling at her angrily.

'If the cap fits...' she remarked, walking out and going to her room.

How she managed to get into these arguments with him she just didn't know. It was perfectly true that she did not argue with anyone else and the last person she wanted to quarrel with was Matthew.

It would be better when this was all over. He had been very prickly with her lately, she mused. His manner had certainly changed. He was not quite as forgiving as he had been. It all boiled down to her previous conclusions. She and Matthew Trevelyan were utterly incompatible.

Next day he left her strictly alone. When she got up he had already left the house and there was a note and a key on the kitchen table. She could let herself in and out as she chose. He had taken her words to heart and Sophie didn't know whether to feel smug or unhappy. It meant that she wouldn't see him all day, probably not until tomorrow morning.

Andrew brought her back that evening and she felt very churlish when she found herself avoiding his goodnight kiss.

'You're different, Sophie,' he complained. 'Living down there has done something to you.'

'Of course it hasn't,' she protested, trying to be breezy. 'And I wish you wouldn't say "down there"; I'm in Cornwall, not hell.'

'That's a debatable point if the man I saw standing at the door when you got back here last night is anything to go by. He looked as if he'd come from down below on a blast of flame. I assume that was the great Matthew Trevelyan—the one that's no relation to you?'

She nodded guiltily and bit her lip. It was very true that when Matthew was annoyed the dark, clever face looked decidedly devilish, and he had been annoyed last night. He would be annoyed tonight too if he was in and realised that she was sitting here with Andrew. The thought made her almost jump. What was she implying? Matthew wasn't jealous, in spite of the odd things he had said the night that he had kissed her.

'Yes, that was Matthew,' she managed lightly. 'He was annoyed as a matter of fact. I hadn't let him know I would be out all day.'

'So he was coming the heavy uncle, or is it just that he fancies you himself?' Andrew asked sarcastically, and Sophie collected her things and prepared to depart.

'I can do without that sort of remark,' she told him coolly. 'I don't expect it from you, Andy. I have problems enough as it is without trouble from my friends.'

He was very contrite but his words had unsettled her more than ever, and when she went into the house she was almost relieved to find that Matthew was not there. He didn't come in either—at least, not while she was awake—and Sophie assumed that he would be at some very splendid dinner—the sort that writers of his class were always attending.

He would have been doing special things, being important, laughing with people whom she would never even meet. And what had she been doing? She had been with Esther, trying on clothes and doing bits for the wedding—being ordinary in other words. She tossed in bed and pondered miserably on the fact that she was not anything like Matthew.

CHAPTER EIGHT

NEXT morning Matthew was there. Sophie was up quite early to get ready and she was having breakfast when he came into the room. He was back to being normal—whatever that was—because he smiled at her.

'So, today's the big day? Got all your finery ready?'

'Yes. I brought my dress back last night. My flowers arrived half an hour ago.'

'Do I get to take you today?' he enquired quizzically, and she looked up at him quickly.

'I'll be in a long dress so that would be nice. If it's no trouble?'

'What's trouble between you and me, Sophie?' he asked derisively. 'Don't we thrive on trouble? Just let me know what time you're supposed to leave and I'll be ready.'

She told him the time of the wedding and where the church was and left him to work out the departure time himself. Then she had the whole morning to potter about, have a perfumed bath, paint her nails and try to do something with her curly hair. When he tapped on her door and enquired about lunch she muttered that she didn't want any. She was too tense to eat because sooner or later she would have to step through the door in her bridesmaid's dress and face him, and she felt ridiculously shy about that.

In the end it couldn't be put off any longer because he warned her that they would have to set off and she took one last, anxious look at herself and prepared to face the strange amber gaze.

Esther had chosen a soft green chiffon for Sophie's dress. It made a perfect contrast to her hair and the whole effect was misty, almost unreal. A spray of creamy gardenias was threaded into her bright hair, and as she faced Matthew her anxiety made her purple eyes over-large in her face.

For a second he just looked at her. When she had come out of her room he had been standing with the car keys in his hand, looking slightly impatient, but it was obvious that any hard thoughts he had been having had now left his mind.

His glance slid over her, touching her slender figure in the dreamy dress, lingering on the cream of the flowers in her fiery hair and then moving over her rather pale face and anxious eyes.

'You beautiful little creature,' he said softly. 'I really feel sorry for the bride.'

Sophie didn't know what to say; her eyes were locked with the unswervingly intense golden stare and her heart was beating so rapidly that she felt quite distressed. Shivers seemed to be racing over her skin, her feelings so strong that it was almost frightening. She wanted Matthew to gather her up again but she knew that if he did she would certainly faint. There was no way that she could speak, and his eyes narrowed at her expression.

'Let's go,' he urged quietly. 'There's sure to be a lot of traffic today and I want to get you there in good time.'

'Am I making you miss anything?' she managed nervously, and he gave a sudden laugh that was almost harsh.

'Nothing that I care to mention. Let's go!'

When they arrived at the church she was not pleased to find that quite a lot of people were hanging around at the gate. One of them was Andrew and he had the car door open for her before Matthew could even move.

'You look ravishing!' he announced. He glanced in at Matthew. 'Another guest?' he asked, and Sophie could almost feel Matthew's temper start to rise. He had been silent on the way here except for checking that she had everything with her in a quite gentle way. But there was something goading about Andrew, and one thing that nobody with any wish to survive would do was goad Matthew Trevelyan.

'Matthew is too busy to come,' she said rapidly, and this didn't help at all.

'Good. I'll have you to myself,' Andrew announced loudly, and Sophie felt as if she was in between two battling male animals, one of whom would be insulted because he had no desire to have her to himself. She turned woebegone eyes on Matthew as he stood and watched the events icily from the other side of the car.

'I—I've told you where the reception is...' she began anxiously, and his eyes slid over her face very comprehensively.

'I'll be there, don't worry,' he assured her quietly. 'I know the time.'

'Is he just going to hang around and wait for you?' Andrew asked sharply as the car pulled away. 'I thought he was too busy to bother? Or is a quiet wedding beneath his dignity?'

'Oh, shut up!' Sophie snapped. Talk about green-eyed monsters! she thought. And she was quite sure that Andy would have at least two current girlfriends. His was a very deplorable male attitude and it was embarrassing. Matthew had noticed for sure. As to a 'quiet wedding', there seemed to be hundreds of people here, not one of them as splendid as Matthew. He had been wearing a grey suit and with the darkness of his hair and skin he had looked wonderful. His face seemed to stay in her thoughts all the time.

Luckily she had plenty to do, being the chief bridesmaid, and for a while she concentrated on her duties. Her old self-assurance came back and it was only when the wedding was well under way that she realised how she changed whenever Matthew was near. By herself she was quite a formidable character in her own right— bad luck and viruses apart. When Matthew was near, though, she just changed. Either she wanted to fight him or fall at his feet.

She was busy all the time at the reception. It was held at a hotel close to Esther's home, and when Esther threw her bouquet Sophie was at great pains not to catch it. In fact she dodged it to such an extent that everyone noticed and laughed at her.

It made her the focus of all eyes for a while and she didn't notice that Matthew had arrived.

'So what are you going to do now?' Patrick asked as he stood with his arm around the bride before they went to get changed. 'There's no need to go back to Cornwall, Sophie. You can have my place. It's paid for for a couple of months and I'll be elsewhere——'

He was speaking quite loudly and Andrew suddenly interrupted. 'Lower your voice when you speak to Sophie,' he remarked in a quite biting manner. 'Her devil's just arrived.'

Everyone was puzzled except Sophie, and when she looked up Matthew was standing quite close. Patrick didn't seem capable of taking a hint.

'What about it?' he continued. 'You could be back in London with your friends and no rent to pay for a while. It beats the wilds of Cornwall.'

It was exactly what she had been hoping to arrange, but that now seemed to have been ages ago and she didn't know what to say.

'Go on, Sophie,' Andrew urged. 'We can get back together again. All this distance is forcing us apart. I'm hoping that the next wedding will be ours.'

She would never have believed it of him. She knew quite well that he was saying this so that Matthew would hear. It made her quite tongue-tied with embarrassment. Not that she had to say anything at all, because Matthew was beside her even though she hadn't noticed him move.

'Sophie is with me,' he said coldly. 'If she wants a place in London she can have my place on a permanent, no-rent basis.'

He looked at her, towering over her, and his hand came firmly to her arm in that proprietorial manner of his, but she didn't mind at all, although she had the feeling that he would tell her to say thank you nicely if she didn't get control of her tongue.

'Yes, that's true,' she assured Patrick, forcing a smile to her trembling lips. 'Thanks all the same, Patrick. In any case, all my things are in Cornwall.'

'Things can be moved,' Andrew said angrily. 'When you went down there I didn't imagine that you would be a prisoner. I expected to see you.'

'Visit us,' Matthew offered silkily, and Andrew looked a little taken aback.

'Visit you?' he asked in a stunned voice, and Matthew gave him a smile that did not in any way reach his eyes.

'Certainly,' he said smoothly. 'Any time at all before September.' He looked down at Sophie. 'I take it that your duties are finished? When the bride and groom drive off so will we.'

'But there's the rest of the day,' Andrew began, and he got the same cold smile.

'Not for Sophie,' Matthew informed him. 'The devil has come to claim his own.'

That little remark made even Andrew look uncomfortable because it was obvious that Matthew had heard his earlier words. From that moment Matthew's hand didn't leave Sophie's arm until she was ready to go.

Luckily it was not too long because, in reality, everything was over in spite of Andrew's comments to the contrary. Sophie was glad that Matthew had not come sooner. Esther was staring at him in stunned admiration, Patrick was looking at him suspiciously and Andrew was simply glaring at everyone. She was very relieved to get away finally and be tucked up into Matthew's car.

'Well, well,' he murmured sardonically as he drove off. 'Everyone's fighting over you, Lady Sophrina.'

'I never noticed,' she said quickly, and he shot her a very derisive glance.

'Really?' he enquired drily. 'There was Esther's husband trying to accommodate you, Andrew like a dog about to lose his bone, and then, of course, there was me. That makes three men fighting over you—two of them quite obviously ready to do real battle.'

'I'm quite sure that Patrick...' Sophie began in an embarrassed voice, and he laughed quite grimly.

'I wasn't actually thinking of Esther's husband,' he assured her cynically. 'Newly wed is perhaps a bit too soon.'

Well, that left Andrew and—and Matthew. She could not imagine Matthew being prepared to battle over her; he only battled *with* her. He was taunting her again, although he looked quite annoyed.

'You're being nasty,' she complained quietly, and he nodded as if he was giving it some thought.

'True,' he agreed in a more mocking manner. 'Put it down to the fact that I've discovered that you take a lot of watching.'

'You don't have to watch me,' she protested, and he shot her a very taunting glance before his lips twisted in a caustic smile.

'Is that a fact?' he enquired, and she decided to follow her own advice to Andrew and shut up.

Matthew's annoyance was gone by the time they reached Kensington, however, and as they went inside the house he asked her what she would like to do.

'Do you want a night on the town, an early night or would you like to go back to Trembath?' he asked as they stepped into the hall. It gave Sophie something to think about. She would have liked to say, All three, but then again she was not in any sort of state to face Matthew's world. The rather fierce male attitudes that had surfaced at the wedding had somewhat unnerved her.

'A quiet meal?' she asked warily, looking up at him, and Matthew contemplated her rather anxious face for a second.

'Fine. Before that you can show me where you used to live.'

'I'm sure you wouldn't be interested,' she said quickly, but the black brows rose enquiringly.

'Not interested? Or course I am. It will nicely occupy our time until we eat.'

'We could just—just stay here until then,' she ventured, but his glance swept over her like a strike of lightning.

'We couldn't, really we couldn't,' he assured her ironically. 'Change into something less enchanting and we'll go now.'

Sophie had to admit that he was wise. There was a lot of tension crackling between them and staying in the small house at the moment was not a good idea. She could only hope that an excursion would clear the air.

After a while it did, especially as Matthew had to get out of the car and pace about in front of her previous dwelling. It looked particularly sad at the moment because they had already started to pull down the row, although the house where she had lived was still standing. Matthew stood and frowned at it blackly and then got back into the car.

'And what sort of place are you planning on occupying while you're at college?' he enquired in a voice that dared her to suggest anything other than a luxury flat. 'The chance of you being able to get accommodation in college is nil.'

'There are plenty of places in London,' she assured him with an effort at being carefree.

'What places?' he demanded. 'You're a twenty-three-year-old woman, not a student in knee socks. You need a secure and comfortable place if you're going to study and make up all this lost time you've created.'

'I didn't create it!' Sophie protested, and he shot her a wry look.

'From the information I was given at the time, your turbulent character created it. That, however, is neither here nor there. Back to the accommodation.'

'There's ages yet,' she reminded him. 'I'll think about it later.'

'Yes,' Matthew said grimly. 'But if you think about anything resembling the place I've just seen you can crush the thought at birth. It seems to me that staying in my London place would make sound sense.'

'What?' She turned sideways in her seat to stare at him in amazement. 'But it—it's your place! You said it was your pad, a sort of refuge.' She couldn't believe this. He was acting as if he cared about her and yet he had distinctly said that she was just a ship passing in the night.

'You're not going to be at university for the rest of your life,' he growled. 'I expect to get it back if you borrow it. As to me, I've more or less decided to go back to America for a while.'

'Oh.' Sophie sat in silence, thoughts colliding in her head. She wouldn't see him. He would be thousands of miles away. What about Pip? Would he take Pip with him?

'Will you take Pip with you?' she asked, almost in a whisper, and Matthew shot her a glance that changed from annoyance to thoughtfulness when he saw her expression.

'Why do you care so much about my son?' he enquired softly.

'I suppose because he reminds me a bit of me at that age, except that maybe I wasn't so tough. I just thought I was.' She looked out of the window and avoided his probing gaze. 'Sometimes it was hard, and I can't help imagining Pip at school and——'

'Will it settle your mind if I promise to talk it over with you?' he asked, and she was again looking at him in amazement.

'You mean it? But why? I—I'll be gone and you said that——'

'I've said a lot of things,' Matthew agreed. 'Let's just put it down to the fact that you've made an impression on me.' He stared rather grimly through the windscreen and concentrated on driving. 'It's a little like having a conscience living in the same house—a determined conscience in glowing Technicolor. Ignoring you is impossible.'

He didn't say anything else and Sophie kept quiet. He had given her so many things to think about and now she was feeling very guilty. There was this business of her money. She could have told him then but she had missed the opportunity and now Matthew had become silent and grim. The next chance she got she would bring the matter up. In any case, all this talk had brought home to her the fact that her time with him was very limited. If he went to America it would be final.

They had dinner at a very quiet place and Matthew told her that this was where he ate most evenings when he came to London. It was difficult to make conversation and Sophie had the feeling that it was as difficult for him as it was for her. Somehow this day had changed things on a quite permanent basis. It had in some way altered her relationship with him. There was this feeling in the air and they were both on edge.

It had also altered her relationship with Andrew, she realised, because she had seen him in a very bad light. He had simply been flexing his masculinity with Matthew and had come off a bad second. Who wouldn't with Matthew? She looked up at him in the soft light of the restaurant, her eyes roaming over his face. She should never have taken up his offer of rescue. It would have been better if she had never met him again, because she was utterly captivated.

He turned his head, his eyes meeting hers, an intensity about his gaze that brought colour to her cheeks, and his face tightened as she looked away hastily.

'Let's go,' he ordered abruptly, signalling for the waiter, and Sophie knew it was because he had read her look very well. He just wanted out of all this and she could hardly blame him. She was certainly an uncalled-for complication in his life.

She went off to her room and stayed there when they got back to the house. She would keep out of his way from now on. More and more he seemed to be feeling that he should take care of her and she had never intended that. In any case, it was unbearable to feel that she was a burden to him.

*   *   *

When they returned to Cornwall Sophie knew at once that things could not go on as they had before. The atmosphere had changed completely and she realised that her time here would have to end soon. There was no possibility of her staying at Trembath House until September.

It meant that lots of things would be left undone— most of all her promise to alter Pip's schooling arrangements and make him more happy. It would never do now, though, to have a fight with Matthew. In the first place she didn't at all feel like it, and in the second place she now felt very nervous in his presence.

For a while she tried to avoid him. He went back to work the moment they arrived and seemed determined to stay in his study as long as possible each day. He even stopped taking his morning swim and the only time she saw him was when he joined her for dinner. On these occasions he was so very polite and noncommittal that she was glad to escape to her room afterwards. She got a great deal of work done herself, which was exactly what she had intended to do in the first place.

She began to think that this would go on indefinitely, until one evening Matthew announced that they would be dining out again. Sophie was not too surprised. Since she had been staying at Trembath House Eve had not been near the place and she assumed that her presence would have put quite a strain on Mrs Corwin's relationship with Matthew, whatever that was.

And this time she made no attempt to captivate anyone at all. Not in any way would she allow Matthew to think that she was jealous about his relationship with Eve, and in any case she just wanted to fade into the background. However, there was not much chance of that.

'Ah! The beautiful Sophrina!' Brad greeted her as they walked into the restaurant. Eve was standing at the bar; the greeting antagonised her at once and she instantly attached herself to Matthew, hanging on his arm and speaking to him in a low voice that cut Sophie out completely. She had no alternative but to talk to Brad until their table was ready, and that seemed to annoy Eve too.

It was a no-win situation, Sophie mused, especially as she looked up suddenly and found Matthew's amber eyes on her in such an icy manner that she had to search her mind rapidly for some fault. Dinner, under the circumstances, was not exactly a great success, especially as Brad hung around for a good deal of the time, asking her about her trip to London and saying that he would have loved to see her in her bridesmaid's dress.

'Did you go to this wedding, Matt?' Eve asked in a way that said she would be surprised if he had lowered his dignity to attend such an insignificant affair, and Matthew shook his head.

'A few minutes only, to collect Sophie. Weddings do not appeal to me.' He said it coldly and Sophie felt herself shrink inside. He would never forget Delphine. Even now he was probably wishing that they had not come here because the conversation had taken this turn.

'I suppose you stayed with your friends in London?' Eve enquired, looking at Sophie, but before she could reply Matthew did it for her.

'She stayed with me. I have a house in London, and naturally Sophie stayed there.'

'Wasn't that rather risking her reputation?' Brad asked, with a knowing look that had Sophie's cheeks flaring.

'Don't be ridiculous! She's his niece!' Eve snapped shrilly, glaring at both her husband and Sophie, but Matthew had a line in icy looks that finally sent both of them on their way.

'Sophie is not my niece,' he ground out. 'As for her reputation, it will be perfectly safe providing that people mind their own business and leave us to mind ours.'

He did not actually speak to Sophie again, and this time when the meal was over he did not linger at the bar either. When they were back in the car and driving to the house Sophie felt she had to say something.

'I'm sorry you were angry,' she ventured quietly. 'I seem to have caused a lot of trouble in your life.'

'Don't blame yourself for other people's stupidity,' he grated, adding more softly, 'In any case, there are undercurrents there that you know nothing about.'

Sophie kept quiet. She would have had to be blind not to know about the undercurrents. Eve wanted Matthew and Brad liked playing at being the Lothario. There wasn't much to choose between them as far as she could see.

'Keep away from Brad Corwin,' Matthew growled, and that really surprised her.

'I'm not exactly likely even to see him,' she pointed out. 'I never go out unless you're there. In any case, you know I don't like him. I don't like either of them.'

This time he did not remind her that they were his friends. Instead he was silent for a minute and then said, 'If you want to go anywhere, Sophie, you only have to tell me.'

'I—I'm happy where I am,' she muttered. 'It's a change from the bustle of London. It's like a holiday.'

'Can you drive?' he asked, and she looked across at him with a smile.

'Yes. When I first went to London I had huge plans. I also had a bit of money. I took lessons and sometimes drove Andrew's car. I'm a bit rusty now but I think I can say that I drive.'

'We should perhaps get you going again,' he murmured. 'That way you'll have a bit more freedom when I'm not here.'

Sophie went very still. It seemed to be a hint that he was going away. Pip would be back for the end of term in a month. Was Matthew going away soon? She didn't dare to ask. She was still trying not to beg him to stay when he parked the car in front of the house and got out to come round to her.

'Let's walk on the beach,' he suggested quietly. 'It's not cold tonight and you seem to be dressed more warmly than you were last time we dined out in Port Withian.'

Sophie grimaced to herself. He'd probably meant nothing by that remark but she still remembered making a fool of herself that last time. Tonight she had put on a warm woollen dress, and although it was smart it was not designed to allure. She had a coat on too and she was happy to agree to a walk on the beach. She didn't want to go to her room and not see Matthew again tonight.

They went down one of the cliff paths. It was quite an easy walk because, although there was a sheer drop close to the house, there were several places where the beach was easily accessible. Sophie had been there with Pip and it was no surprise to her.

The tide was out and when she glanced at the water Matthew calmed any fears she might have had.

'It's exactly slack-water. At this time the sea is as far away as it's going to get.'

'I expect you know all the tides,' Sophie mused. 'Living in this house you would know the sea.'

'I know it. Anyone in Cornwall who lives by the sea knows it. The sea here is not a thing to be taken casually and I hope you'll remember that.'

He took her arm as they walked along and gradually Sophie relaxed. It was peaceful. For once the sea was calm, almost whispering. When she mentioned this Matthew laughed.

'Slack-water. I told you. Give it a while and it will come raging back.'

'I think I would be scared to be here alone at night,' she murmured as the moon came out and shone across the sand. It seemed to make the dark places darker still, the rocks more stark, and under the height of the cliffs she could see caves. She had never been to this part with Pip. 'I would be expecting smugglers, or more probably ghosts of smugglers.'

'Well, according to local folklore, these caves were hiding places for contraband in the past. If any ghosts were hanging about they would certainly be here.'

'Do you think so?' Sophie felt a cold shiver and moved closer to him and Matthew laughed down at her.

'Scaring yourself again?' he asked in amusement. Actually she was, but nothing could scare her as much as the idea that Matthew would go away. She would have faced any ghost in order to walk here with him by the sea in the moonlight. At least, she thought so until there was a whoosh of sound and some night bird flew out from the cliff and skimmed dangerously close to her face.

With a little scream she hurled herself at Matthew and was caught instantly in two strong arms. He held her fast, and when she had enough courage to look up he was grinning at her.

'Oh, Sophie,' he teased. 'You're just about one of the oddest people I know. I'm never even sure how old you are. Sometimes you're just like a child.'

'I'm not, though.' She looked up at him. In the moonlight her eyes looked dark, almost black, and the light darkened her fiery hair, taking away the flames and leaving only the dark shine. The light made Matthew look even more dark, like a phantom from the past, a midnight caller to lure her away from safety, a pirate from long ago.

And she would go if he lured her, she thought. If he called she would simply follow, even if he called from a long way off. She gazed up at him and the teasing smile died on his lips as he looked down at her.

'Don't!' he ordered sharply, and she just went on looking at him.

'I'm not doing anything,' she whispered, and his hands tightened on her shoulders, biting into her through the warmth of her coat.

'Oh, yes, you are,' he assured her harshly. 'You're standing there like a slave—submissive, docile, waiting for your fate.'

The words and the hard tone shocked her and Sophie gave a little murmur of distress, trying to pull away from his grasp, but it was too late. He unbuttoned her coat, his hands closed round the warmth of her body, and the breath left her throat at the power of his kiss as his lips closed over hers.

'You're like dark velvet,' he breathed against her mouth. 'Down here by the sea nothing is real; nothing matters except holding you, tasting you.'

She was powerless in his arms and even if he had let her go she would still have stayed there. His kisses covered her face and throat and she wrapped her arms around his neck, joyfully accepting everything. He was right. Nothing else mattered. Everything else was quite unreal. There was just this moment, the dark moonlight, the sound of the sea, and Matthew.

He lifted his head but she gave a soft, demanding little cry and reached up to him and he caught her close again, his lips devouring her until she could think of nothing else. Flares of heat ran over her skin and her arms tightened round his neck as he molded her close to him.

He wanted her. His body hardened against her soft curves and Sophie began to kiss him back frantically, every part of her alive with excitement, her breathing uneven, her heart racing under his hand.

It was Matthew who stopped the moonlit madness. He held her close in a way that was almost trapping her, tightening his hold on her head when she protested and struggled to kiss him again.

'Enough, Sophie,' he ordered softly. 'Enough.' The sound of his voice was like a reprimand and she gave a mournful little cry. It was frustration and dismay all mixed together and he heard it very well.

'No,' he whispered against her face. 'Don't start blaming yourself for this too. I never meant it to happen but it did and I should have known better. It stops here, though, Sophie.'

'I—I didn't mean to...' Matthew was so important to her that she found herself trying to explain her actions away even though he had told her it was no fault of hers, and he gave her a gentle little shake.

'You did nothing at all,' he insisted. 'I brought you here. It was all my idea and I was the one who initiated this. Now it's time to stop.'

'Why?' she asked mournfully, and for a second his face darkened with something very like anger before he saw the bewildered look in her eyes.

'Have you ever felt like that before?' he asked softly, and when she shook her head he took her face in his hands and looked into her eyes. 'Then you have about as much experience as I imagined when I first saw you, and that's why we have to stop.'

He did not allow any sort of dissent. Almost before she knew it, Sophie was being helped up the track to the garden and it seemed like only a few dreamy minutes before they were back at the house and standing in the hall.

Once in the light she felt too shy to look at him, and he understood that because he refused to let her simply run away. He took her hand and made her go with him to the sitting-room and she found herself seated on the settee while he poured her a drink.

'Brandy for shock,' he remarked as he handed it to her, and her small, reproachful look served only to amuse him. After a second, though, his amusement died and he looked at her seriously. 'I have to leave, Sophie,' he said quietly.

Her head shot up and he shrugged as he saw her distressed face. 'Damn it all, Sophie, you know I have to,' he insisted almost savagely. 'This state of affairs can't go on. It's been growing since you came here. I'm fascinated by everything about you; I want to keep you here and not even let you out.'

He turned away with angry impatience. 'This is not me. I'm behaving like a lunatic. I hate your friends merely because they know you. I want you for myself and I have no right to feel like that about Quentin's daughter.'

She felt joy almost choking her but there was a slight fear too because Matthew's dark face was alive with an emotion that she had never seen before in her life.

'But—but if you love me . . .' she began, and he spun round to look at her, his eyes blazing with that peculiar amber light.

'I said I want you,' he grated. 'I want you in my bed; I want to sleep with you, to own you. That is not love. That is physical desire.'

At that moment Sophie could not look away and Andrew's words came unbidden into her mind. He had called Matthew her devil. Right now he looked like that and she managed to make her trembling legs stand.

'You don't have to go away,' she said shakily. 'I can go.' He started to speak, but she held up her hand and to her surprise he let her talk first. 'I think I'm going to get the money that was left to me,' she told him quickly. 'The business I had in London was seeing the solicitor and he seems to think they can't keep it now that I'm going to college. It's grown in four years, too, and I'll have enough to see me through with no difficulty. So, you see, *I'll* be able to go.'

'No!' Matthew almost shouted the denial and he was across to her in two strides. 'I've brought this on with my obsession. You're safe here. Biddy will probably agree to sleep in and you can get your work done.' He suddenly realised that once again he was demanding, and his expression softened. 'Stay here,' he said quietly. 'I write better in London anyway and I'll know where you are.'

For a moment she looked up at him and then she nodded and sat down again. She was not going to start behaving like a lovesick girl. If Matthew could be so businesslike then so could she.

'Very well,' she agreed calmly. 'There really is no need, though. I've already told you that I have plans for my future. I intend to go to university and make a life from there.' She took a sip of brandy, almost choking at the fiery liquid. 'What about Pip?' she asked. 'In just under a month he'll be here for half-term.'

'Then I'll be back,' Matthew muttered, as if it hadn't come into his mind until she'd mentioned it. 'If you want to stay in London during that time...'

'I do not,' she informed him sharply. 'I promised Pip I would help him, and *you* told me you would discuss it with me.'

'Oh, God, Sophie! Don't you ever stop?' he groaned, his hand coming across his eyes. 'I do not want to discuss my son at this moment.'

'Tomorrow, then,' she insisted.

'Tomorrow I'm leaving,' he told her, and she tightened her lips to stop the cry of denial that rose from her throat. She got to her feet and made for the door.

'Before you leave, then,' she insisted, and his tense stance suddenly relaxed as he turned to look at her.

'Do you ever give in?' he enquired with soft mockery, but Sophie wanted to get out. She was not quite sure whether or not she was going to cry.

'No,' she stated flatly. 'I don't.'

CHAPTER NINE

SOPHIE didn't cry after all because she had the overwhelming feeling that she belonged here, that she belonged to Matthew, and in a way it took much of the sadness out of things. The sensation lent a good deal of strength to her approach to him the next day and immediately after breakfast she went to find him. He had skipped the meal, and she could understand that, but he had made a promise and he was going to keep it.

When she knocked on his study door he was busy packing his books and papers and he looked up at her rather warily. 'We were going to discuss Pip,' she announced firmly, and he motioned her to a seat before walking round to sit on the edge of his desk.

'All right,' he agreed tightly. 'As there seems to be no escape I may as well get it over with.'

'You made the offer in the first place,' she reminded him severely. 'Basically, it's nothing to do with me and normally I wouldn't dream of interfering.'

He stared at her with an inflexibility that would previously have unnerved her. She held her ground, however, because there was still this feeling of belonging, of destiny.

'Normality seems to be a thing of the past,' he stated grimly. 'You're about to make demands that in my right mind I would refuse with a good deal of annoyance.'

'You probably will now,' she countered, 'but I made a promise too, and I'm not backing down without a fight.'

Matthew threw up his hands and began to pace about.

'Sophie! This has nothing to do with you at all.' He turned to frown at her frustratedly. 'I'm too damned soft with you!'

'Why?' She asked the question very quietly and he just stopped in his tracks and looked at her for a second before walking round to sit in his chair.

He didn't answer her. Instead he said, 'Right! Let's have it.'

'Why can't Pip be at a day-school closer to home?' she asked seriously. 'I know that at the moment he's perhaps a bit obsessed by the uncalled-for behaviour of the games master, but basically he's only a little boy and I think he would be happy going to school each day from here.'

'It's not quite as simple as that,' Matthew pointed out, looking at her seriously. 'Sometimes I'm away for a day or two. What does he do then? How does he get home at night? Who looks after him?'

'Biddy,' Sophie said promptly. 'Most of these day-schools have a school bus now as far as I can tell. He could be dropped off at night and Biddy would be here. I don't suppose you're away all that much.'

'And suppose there is no school bus?' he persisted.

'We could look for a place that did have a school bus and then, all other things being equal...'

'*We*?' he asked softly. 'Aren't you taking your role as Pip's friend a little too seriously?' He was looking at her steadily and she fought down the desire to look away.

'A figure of speech,' she explained breezily. 'If you wanted any help in looking then of course I would help you, providing it wasn't in the too distant future. Remember I'll be off to London at the end of August.'

'I haven't forgotten,' he grated, standing and coming round the desk. 'I'll give it some thought, and now, if you don't mind, I have quite a lot to do before I leave.'

'When are you going?' she wanted to know.

Her heart fell when he said, 'As soon as I can get my things into the car.' She didn't comment, and he looked across at her, catching the lost expression on her face. 'Fate isn't particularly kind, Sophie,' he pointed out quietly. 'It hasn't been kind to either of us.'

'Well, I intend to change my fate,' she stated with almost tearful vehemence. She turned to the door, but he called to her and she stopped although she did not turn round. She felt that she could not look at him at the moment.

'What do you need before I go?' he asked, and she stiffened at the gentleness in his voice.

'Nothing. I told you, I'll probably get my money.' She turned then, a sort of mournful defiance in her face. 'When I do I shall leave. I shall go back to London and settle in early for the term. Keep in touch or you may find that I've gone when you get back.'

For a moment he looked seriously angry, and then he gave her a quizzical smile as he walked towards her.

'Somehow I don't think so. I rather imagine that your little ghosts and the pull of the wild sea will keep you here.' He stood close and smiled down at her. 'In fact, disgraceful though it may seem, I'm rather banking on it.'

'Then why don't you stay?' she asked breathlessly, and his eyes darkened as he took her face in his hands.

'You know damned well why,' he said tightly. 'Now get out of here and let me get out too. There's no future in this insanity and I am not about to seduce Quentin's daughter.'

He gave her a push towards the door and Sophie went, admitting defeat. Actually, she mused as she paced about her own room, she had not won anything at all. He had only promised to think about moving Pip and she was losing him because he had strong convictions. As a matter of fact she had never had him to lose, she reminded herself. He was attracted to her because she looked like her grandmother and it was all hopeless because he still loved Delphine.

Biddy moved into the house on a temporary basis and didn't seem to mind that she was being inconvenienced at all. She would do anything for Matthew, Sophie realised. How was it that he had everybody falling over themselves to accommodate him when he was just the devil with a soft, dark voice? And she was no exception either. She missed him so much that for a while she watched each morning to see if he might have come back and gone for his swim.

There was, as he had said, no future in such lunacy and she settled down to her work vigorously—so vigorously in fact that if Biddy had not intervened with persistent regularity she wouldn't have left the house at all. She rang Mr Brown, and after a lot of skirting around the subject he told her that the bank was considering the matter and would be in touch with her.

His tone was quite clear—she was to stop pestering him, and Sophie was not at all pleased. She had not pestered him enough in the past—she realised that now. Not that it mattered. She would not have come to Cornwall if she had not been desperate, and if she had not come she would never have met Matthew. Whatever finally happened, she would never regret that.

Now that he had gone the feeling of inevitability was somewhat tempered by dread. It was, after all, merely in her imagination that she belonged here, and she had to admit that if Matthew did not belong here too then she was not at all sure she wanted to be at Trembath.

It all boiled down to the fact that she loved him, and when she finally admitted that to herself she felt a surge of panic about her future. She had never felt love before and had never known the great empty hole it left inside when the other person felt nothing of the sort. The fright made her work harder than ever and the time passed by.

Two weeks later she had a letter from the bank. She was to be allowed to have the money and she could have it at once. All she had to do was fill in the enclosed forms and the money would be transferred to her account. There was much more than she had anticipated and Sophie completed the forms immediately. It was better to get things over with because she knew that when Matthew came back nothing would have changed and she would have to go long before the end of August.

She was so intent on getting her affairs in order that she set off to the village to post the forms that same afternoon, even though Biddy warned her that there was a chance of a storm. At least it got her out of the house, and as she walked back from Port Withian later Sophie was glad that she had dealt with things promptly. Now she would no longer be a burden to Matthew.

The wind was blowing quite strongly as she climbed to the headland, and although the sky was still blue the sea was tossing a little more wildly and she assumed that the storm that Biddy had forecast would be there before nightfall. She was beginning to be able to read the weather signs herself now and she even felt the new chill that blew from the sea.

Halfway up the road she had to step into the side to allow a car to pass. But it did not pass and when she looked down at the open window she saw that the face grinning out at her was that of Brad Corwin.

'All lost and lonely?' he asked, eyeing her with amusement.

'Neither,' Sophie told him pertly. 'I've been to post a letter and now I'm walking back. I've been very busy and the walk has done me good—blown a few cobwebs away.'

'You've not been down to have dinner for a while,' he reminded her, and her heart sank as he got out of the car and prepared to make conversation.

'Well, Matthew's in London and I'm more than happy with Biddy's cooking,' she stated.

'So you're all alone in Trembath House?' She didn't like his speculative look and she answered very quickly.

'Of course not! Matthew would never allow that. Biddy is sleeping in until he comes back.'

'You should have let me know. I could have given you a few trips out. I often have to go to Launceston, shopping. I don't suppose Matt takes you very far?'

'We're both extremely busy,' she insisted. She tried to look businesslike. 'I really must be off. I have loads to do before dinner.'

'Jump in. I'll take you back.'

Sophie hesitated. It would, perhaps, be insulting to refuse but she didn't like the look in his eyes and she had no idea either why he was driving up this way, unless he had spotted her in the village and followed. This road led exactly nowhere except on to the moors. In fact very little traffic came past Trembath House at this time of the year. Biddy had already told her that.

'Oh, I'm really enjoying the walk,' she managed, with a bright smile, but just as she thought she was about to get away with it the first drops of rain began to fall.

He looked at her sceptically, everything about him telling her that she was trapped unless she wanted a scene.

'You'll be soaked to the skin. You know what the rain's like here—the very wet kind. Hop in and I'll have you at the house in seconds.'

Which was true, she thought. Maybe she was being a little paranoiac about Brad Corwin. Matthew had warned her, and in any case she had very good instincts of her own. All the same, not much could happen to her at this time of the day and so close to home. She got into the car with a certain amount of reluctance that obviously amused him.

It was true that he had her almost at the house in seconds but he didn't venture up the drive. At the entrance he stopped and switched off the engine. By now it was raining steadily but Sophie had her hand on the car door all the same.

'Thank you,' she said politely, pretending to ignore his odd method of getting her to the house.

'Wait a minute,' he urged. 'I'll take you up there. Let's sit and talk for a while.'

He leaned across to her and she shrank back, her hand feeling for the door-catch.

'I really don't have time,' she began, and he found that very amusing too.

'We can make time,' he said. 'Who's to know?'

His arm came round her and she knew that if she didn't move fast she would be trapped in the seat with no chance at all of getting out. What his aim was she didn't know, but she was not about to wait and find out. She opened the door and almost fell out into the road.

'Sophie! Wait a minute!' While she was still trying to keep her balance he was round the car and taking her by the arms. By this time she was in a state of near panic. She pushed him hard and he was no longer pleased.

'You little fool!' he snarled. 'Don't pretend you're an innocent girl.'

He made a grab for her but she wriggled free, and she felt only great relief when she heard a car come tearing up and stop with a loud screaming of brakes. Help had come and she turned her head to show her gratitude, but her face paled at the sight of Matthew. His expression as he got out of his car and came towards them showed nothing but blind rage.

'Get up to the house!' he rasped as his eyes flared over her angrily. 'You're already wet—a little more rain isn't about to make a lot of difference.'

'I offered to take her up there,' Brad said, and Sophie could hardly believe her ears. He was actually grinning, as if she were some sort of panicky idiot, or worse, and she had not the faintest doubt that, whoever came out of this well, it would not be her. Matthew would believe him.

She took to her heels as she saw Matthew turn to Brad and the rain didn't bother her at all; anything would have been better than the fury in those amber eyes. She really felt as if she had called up the devil because that was exactly how he'd looked.

Close to the house, she decided that she could not face Matthew at all. She knew what he would think. He would imagine that she had been for a ride with Brad and that she had got more than she had bargained for. Brad would say anything at all to get out of this and Matthew would take his word. She turned to the path and the beach and just ignored the growing roar of the sea and the steady downpour. As Matthew had said, she was wet already.

This time it was not at all like her walk on the beach with him. She put her head down against the rain and trudged along the sand, ignoring the roar of the waves. Oddly enough the sound didn't even sink in—her head was too full of panic and questions. Why was Matthew back so soon? Pip was not due home for another two weeks.

Mostly, though, she was imagining his anger when he heard a whole series of lies from Brad, because she had no doubt that he would hear just that. He had known the Corwins for a long time. She was the one who would get all the blame and she had never seen him so angry.

It was only when the sea lightly touched her feet that Sophie came to her senses, and she realised that she had no real idea of where she was. She had walked much further than ever before. Each time she had been down here with Pip they had been flying his kite and hadn't ventured far along the beach. She had now come much further than she had walked with Matthew and, looking up, she saw that there were high cliffs beside her. There was no sign at all of a path and she had walked a long way from Trembath House and the safety of the garden.

She turned to go back and her breath caught in her throat at the sight of a boiling sea already hitting the base of the cliff behind her. She was trapped by the tide. She had foolishly wandered on and taken no account at all of the power that she listened to every day and night.

Sophie began to run on. Going back was impossible because although she could wade through the waves for a while she knew that long before she reached any sort of safety the water would be too high. Already she could hear the seething undertow, and if she lost her footing it would be the end of her.

The sight of caves did not frighten her now. There was a much more real danger than that of the ghosts that lurked in her imagination. She dared not enter the caves either, however, because although one of them might just have led to the surface, as she knew some did on this part of the coast, she had no idea which one. Most of them would be under water when the tide was finally fully in.

The rocky outcrops were slippery under her feet and by now the sky was dark with the storm and approaching night. The need for speed and the bad light made her take chances and she gave a cry of pain as her foot slipped on a partly submerged rock and she lost her balance.

She tried to stand but the pain was too bad and she dragged herself away from the water to crouch against the base of the cliff, knowing that she could not now outrun anything. Tears streamed down her face, mingling with the rain. She would never see Matthew again and it would hurt him badly because, like her grandmother, she would have been lost to the sea.

She was soon shivering with cold and the sea was so loud that it drowned out all coherent thought. Sophie assumed that it was her imagination when she heard a voice shouting her name. She peered into the gathering darkness and her heart leapt with joy when she saw Matthew coming towards her. He was coming the way she had been heading and seconds later he caught her in his arms as she struggled to her feet.

'Sophie!' He crushed her against him, his face against her wet hair. 'Thank God you made it this far. Biddy saw you take off down the cliff path.'

He was holding her so tightly that she could hardly speak. 'I was trapped by the tide.' She gasped the words against his chest. She was so wet and cold that she couldn't stop trembling and he swung her up into his arms.

'The tide doesn't quite reach the cliffs here,' he said, turning back the way he had come. 'Just a bit further and you would have been safe. There's an easy path to the top.' He looked down at her as she snuggled against him for warmth and comfort. 'You know by now when storms are due, Sophie. Why did you come down here in the first place?'

'I don't know. I thought you would be angry. I'm sorry.' She turned her wet face against his jacket and he hugged her more warmly to him.

'It doesn't matter,' he said softly. 'You're safe now, sweetheart.'

It was bliss to hear the gentle endearment. Nobody in her whole life had called her that, and in spite of her cold shivers and her aching ankle she felt secure and happy. Matthew was back and it didn't matter why.

He carried her as if she weighed nothing at all, and when they were at last in the garden, the sound of the sea no longer filled with menace, it was difficult to imagine the fright she had had.

They were both soaking wet and Biddy was standing anxiously at the open door as they reached the house.

'Is she all right?' she asked worriedly, and Matthew nodded.

'Just a twisted ankle as far as I can tell. Make her some hot tea, Biddy, and then get ready to go home. There's no need for you to stay tonight; I'm back.'

'Very well, sir. I must say I'll be glad to see my own little cottage but I'll get my son to drive up for me. I've seen enough of wet people for one night.'

They certainly were wet, and by now Sophie was feeling guilty about Matthew carrying her.

'I can manage...' she began, but he simply turned to the stairs and showed no inclination to put her down.

'You can get a hot shower and then we'll talk about how you can manage,' he muttered, and she felt a twinge of unease. In the thrill of having him close she had almost forgotten Brad Corwin. Sooner or later she would have some explaining to do and she wondered just how Brad had wriggled out of the situation.

Matthew took her into her room. By now he looked a good deal more distant than when he had caught her up on the beach.

'Can you manage to get a shower?' he asked, and when she nodded and looked away he turned to the door. 'I'll get changed myself and then bring your tea up.' He was gone straight away and she concluded that trouble could be expected when he returned. She hobbled into her bathroom and closed the door. Now that he knew she was safe Matthew would be quietly fuming, and she just didn't have any good excuse for her behaviour. There was no doubt that he would tell her so.

The warm water stopped her shivering and eased away the pain in her ankle. She was just coming carefully back into her room, towelling her short, bright curls, when Matthew walked in with a cup of hot tea. He too had showered and changed and Sophie pulled her bathrobe tightly round her slender frame before she sat on the edge of the bed and took her tea from him. It was very difficult to face him and for a second she didn't have the courage.

'All right?' he asked quietly, and when she just nodded he came across to her and crouched down. 'Let me see that ankle.' He had her foot in his hand before she could protest and as soon as he touched her she didn't feel like protesting at all because warmth seemed to spread right through her, her skin reacting to the touch of his finger-tips like some erotic signal.

It seemed to be very quiet in the house, the sound of the sea particularly muted. She had already heard a car come to collect Biddy and the feelings that were shooting through her made Sophie shy. Knowing why she felt like this about Matthew was an added stress because she would never let him find out, and she continued to avoid his eyes as he gently probed her ankle.

'It doesn't hurt much now,' she told him huskily. 'I slipped on a wet rock.'

He looked up at her, his hand still on her ankle, and the words she had been dreading came out then. 'Tell me about Brad Corwin,' he commanded quietly. She told him, exactly as it had happened, and she had no idea how open and honest she sounded, how completely lacking in either guile or sophistication. His eyes roamed over her face and a muscle jerked at the side of his mouth. He seemed almost sombre as Sophie looked into the wonderful amber eyes.

'It's true,' she assured him earnestly. 'I don't know what he told you but——'

'He didn't get the chance to tell me anything,' he said grimly. 'I know him too well to waste my time listening.' He stood and began to pace about impatiently. 'In any case, your safety overrides any of his glib tales and you are certainly not safe with him.'

'I—I thought you were friends,' she murmured, and he gave her a wry look as he turned.

'Don't you mean you thought that Eve and I were having an affair?' he asked. 'It didn't take you long to decide on that, did it?' he added when she blushed and looked away.

He took pity on her and came to stand facing her. 'Brad chases every woman his eye falls on and I suppose Eve turned to me in self-defence.' He sighed as she looked up at him with wide eyes. 'I did not accept her generous offer,' he assured her drily, 'so don't look at me like that. For a while she quite fancied spending her time in London with me but I didn't take to the idea at all. I let her pretend but it didn't seem to improve Brad's dubious ways.'

'I didn't know. I suppose I wasn't very nice to her,' Sophie admitted, and he smiled at her guilty expression.

'She probably never noticed. Eve is pretty tough and, as I recall, she wasn't very nice to you. She didn't much like the idea that you were staying with me.' He began to pace about again. 'I don't suppose she missed the fact that I can't keep my eyes off you.'

'She probably didn't understand that you were attracted to me because I'm like my grandmother,' Sophie said quickly, and that stopped his pacing at once.

'*What*?' Matthew spun round and stared at her. 'Do you think I'm mad? Your grandmother died when I was a little boy. How I feel about you is nothing at all to do with Margaret Trevelyan.'

'I—I just thought...' She got shakily to her feet but she didn't get the chance to go anywhere because suddenly he was right in front of her, grasping her shoulders.

'You'd better start believing the evidence of your own eyes, Sophie,' he told her tautly. 'You know perfectly well why I went away.'

'You came back.' She looked up at him and found herself lost in the golden gaze.

'I just turned in this direction. I even left my things behind in London.' His hands moved over her shoulders, moulding the slender bones. 'Rightly or wrongly, I need you, Sophie,' he finished thickly. 'Tonight I thought I'd lost you.'

'I'm sorry if I frightened you,' she whispered. There were tears glistening in her eyes as she saw the pale tension in his face, and his hands slid inside the neck of her robe, his fingers tracing the silken skin of her shoulders.

'You've frightened me since I first saw you,' he said unevenly. 'Too young, too bright and Quentin's daughter. I should have turned you straight round and sent you back to London.' He slid his hands around her neck and tilted her face with his thumbs. 'I even considered it,' he confessed, 'but the urge to see more of you was too strong and pretty soon I couldn't see enough of you. I want you, Sophie. I want you too much to fight it.'

His lips covered hers hungrily and she instantly moved against him. She wanted him too. Maybe her odd life and her tight control on her emotions had stifled her before she had met Matthew, or maybe she hadn't met the right person until now. She had never felt sexual arousal in her life and she was shaken by the depth of her feelings for him.

Her body seemed simply to take over from her mind, and when his questing hands pulled aside her robe and let it slide to the floor she welcomed the warmth of his palms against her flesh. Her breasts seemed to swell towards him, her nipples hard and tight, and he held her away, his eyes devouring her body. In the rose-tinted light of the lamps she seemed to be gilded by soft colour and his face became strained with desire.

'God!' he moaned. 'You're so beautiful.' With one impatient movement he pulled his sweater over his head and brought her close to the silken roughness of his chest, holding her against him as his free hand cupped the swollen mound of her breast, his thumb moving urgently over the hard pink crest.

He bent his head to take the pleasure in his mouth and Sophie gasped as his strong hands forced her to arch against him. Heat was racing through her, a tight pain blossoming, and the tugging at her breast forced a low cry of pain and pleasure from her lips.

'Don't stop me, sweetheart,' he breathed. 'It's already too late to stop. It's been too late since I knew you were safe.'

'I don't want to stop,' she gasped, and he brought her fiercely against his hard body.

When she felt the throbbing arousal of his manhood she opened like a flower and he ran his hand down her back, savouring the feel of her.

'Kiss me,' she moaned. 'Kiss me, Matthew!' And his lips opened over hers with such sweet hunger that Sophie felt faint with pleasure.

She murmured anxiously after a second then tugged at the belt that dug into her soft flesh and he needed no explanations. Still holding her tightly, his lips on hers, he unfastened the belt and slid out of the rest of his clothes, letting her feel the whole of his body against hers for the first time.

His lips were harder, more demanding, and when she put her arms round his neck he brought her sharply against his warmth. Far from terrifying her, his action brought a storm of feeling flooding through her, and she wound herself around him, pressing herself even closer.

His arms seemed to crush her and his original gentleness left him completely at this signal of her need and pleasure. He swung her up into his arms and she felt the softness of the bed beneath her before his powerful body covered her own.

His hand caressed her jawline for a second and then he tilted her face, holding her captive as his mouth moved hungrily over hers. Her lips parted willingly and the heated invasion of his tongue brought her arching towards him urgently. Heat began to flood through her and she was actually afraid that the excitement would kill her.

In the distance she could hear moans of pleasure and realised that they were coming from her, but she wanted much more and she tore her lips away, her cries demanding.

'Sophie! Not yet,' he said in a shaky voice. 'I never expected you to be like this. I can't hurt you.'

'Now! Now!' she begged. 'Please, Matthew!'

His eyes moved over her face like molten gold and even in that moment she was aware of the darkness of his skin, the hard, fine line of his jaw. The shining black hair had fallen over his forehead and her violet eyes grew enormous as it finally sank in that she was actually here with him. She touched his face lightly with trembling fingers, wonder in her expression.

'You're the one who is beautiful,' she whispered. 'Love me now, Matthew, or I'll die.'

'Sophie, my darling,' he murmured huskily, and then he thrust himself into the honeyed warmth of her body.

She gave a sharp cry, and it was all she knew because the room seemed to fade completely away as her body took over and moved with his into another world that cradled her in dark velvet and splintered into ecstasy. Whatever she had expected it had not been this. Her body went into spasms and dimly she heard Matthew gasp with equal pleasure.

She couldn't feel anything but glowing happiness and it was minutes before she realised that her legs were wrapped demandingly around him and that he was holding her almost cruelly tight, his face against her breast. Her skin was burning and so was his, and as Sophie's head fell back and relaxation flooded over her Matthew raised himself carefully and it seemed to break some glittering spell.

Tears filled her eyes and rolled down her cheeks and he looked down at her for a long time before moving on to his side, collecting her and folding her possessively in his arms, letting her cry.

'I'm sorry,' she said after a minute, when the sobbing had been reduced to just a catch in her voice. 'It's not because—I mean you didn't hurt me—I don't know why...'

'It was the first time,' he said softly, but Sophie knew it wasn't only that. What had happened to her would never happen with anyone else. She loved him more than she had ever realised.

CHAPTER TEN

SOPHIE fell asleep in the lamplight, unaware that Matthew had turned his head and was looking down at her with the same sombre expression on his face that she had noticed earlier. His hand touched her cheek and she turned, her arm coming across him as she snuggled closer, and he reached for her, folding her in his arms, protecting her, his eyes staring, unseeing, into the softly lit room.

It was early in the morning when she awoke, and Matthew was not there. She lay for a while, thinking, reliving the night, and at the back of her mind she was unhappy. She knew that he had simply let his desire take over after fighting it before, but it really didn't change much. He still loved Delphine, and even if he wanted her to stay Sophie was not sure she could live with that.

She loved him so much that seeing the memory of another woman in his eyes would destroy her. By now he had probably had time to think too and he would be regretting last night. It was different for him and she was not going to let him think that she would now hang around and expect anything. She had never expected anything in her life.

She went downstairs, forcing herself to face things, just as she had always done. Matthew was in the kitchen and he glanced at her keenly as she walked in. It was the expression she had expected. He regretted last night. His eyes looked darker, almost bruised, and she steeled herself to play a part she had already rehearsed.

168

'Are we too early for Biddy?' she asked brightly, and he turned back to the task he had been doing as she'd walked in.

'Biddy won't be here today,' he told her. 'Apparently she has a very bad cold.'

'How odd,' Sophie managed cheerfully. 'Considering that we were the ones who ended up soaking wet, it hardly seems fair.'

Matthew turned to smile at her and she could tell he was grateful for her blithe chatter. How did other people behave after making passionate love? she wondered. She had no experience to draw on, nothing to tell her how to act.

'I've made breakfast,' he said as he turned to put the tea and toast on the kitchen table. 'If Biddy is going to be off for any length of time we'll have to give some thought to the cooking.'

'I can cook.' Sophie settled at the table and began to pour tea for both of them, making her actions as businesslike as possible. 'I won't be here, though. That was something I was going to talk to you about when you came back but——'

'Events overtook us,' he finished for her in a tense voice.

'Yes.' She felt colour rising in her cheeks and she knew that she had to get this over with very fast. 'While you were away the bank transferred all my legacy into my account. They've accepted that I'm now going to university and really there was no way they could hang on to it.'

Matthew said nothing at all and she dared not look up.

'The money has grown too,' she went on quickly. 'I'll be able to manage very well. I didn't know there was so much.' She looked up then—she had to—and clashed with Matthew's intent gaze. It took more courage than she knew she possessed to look into his eyes. 'That being the case, I don't need to be here and I've decided to go straight back to London. I'll go today.'

'Why the haste?' There was a harshness in his voice but she knew she had to face that.

'It's best to go now. We both know that things...' Sophie choked up and she was grateful when he ignored it.

'You can have my house,' he offered bleakly, but she shook her head.

'No. I don't want to be in any way——'

'Connected to me,' he finished bitterly, and Sophie felt annoyance rising over her misery. She was doing this as much for him as for herself. She knew that he regretted last night and she knew that she would never be able to accept the fact that he still loved Delphine. Even if he had wanted her to stay for the rest of her life the wonder would have been ruined by the ghost of another woman. He must surely know that himself.

'It would be better if you let me finish my own sentences,' she informed him sharply. 'I was going to say that I don't want to feel that I'm your responsibility. I'm grown-up.'

'Oh, I know that. After last night I can't go on having doubts about it.' He looked at her unswervingly, his eyes narrowed now and gleaming like hard amber. 'It was a privilege to be your first lover. Who's going to be the next? Surely not Andrew?'

'I didn't intend the conversation to be like this,' she managed in a low voice. She avoided his eyes. He was hurting her so badly that she felt like jumping up and running from the room. 'I wanted this to be civilised. I thought you would understand. I've always intended to go to university. I told you I had my life planned. And I've been quite a burden to you. Now I'm simply telling you that I won't be a burden any more. I can cope. I can manage. I'm just going to get out from under your feet and let you get on with your life.'

'I appreciate your thoughtfulness. So do I take you to London?' he asked coldly. He got up, abandoning his breakfast, and Sophie did the same. She couldn't face one more minute of this.

'I'm going to get a taxi to the station. When I've got a place to stay I'll send for my things.'

'And immediately?' he rasped. 'What are you about to do in the short term—roam about knocking on doors to see if there's a place to stay?'

'I'll take up Patrick's offer,' she said quietly. There was no way that she was going to be drawn into a fight with him, because she would simply fold up and weep.

'I see,' he said more calmly. 'You don't miss a trick, do you, Sophie? Very self-reliant.'

'I've never had much choice,' she reminded him. 'I learned to survive.'

He stood looking at her for a long time, and then his anger faded and the sombre look she had noticed before came back. He gave a slight smile and nodded.

'You're very wise, Sophie. Of the two of us you probably have more sense. I let my feelings drown me. You recovered. It must be youth.'

He walked out of the room and seconds later she heard his study door close. He did not slam it and that bothered her. She felt as if she had wounded him, that she had found a weak spot and dealt him a mortal blow. When she went back upstairs to her room the first fifteen minutes were spent in crying but at least she had managed not to do that in front of Matthew. He would never know what this gesture was costing her.

She packed her clothes. The rest would have to wait. Maybe Biddy would get them together for her but even if she had to leave them here to be thrown out she could not spend any more time close to Matthew without breaking down and begging to stay.

She had already found the train times, and as the time drew near she phoned for a taxi, praying that one would be available. She thought that at this time of year she would probably be lucky, and she was. It only remained to say goodbye.

She made her face up carefully, erasing all sign of tears. She was leaving things undone. Pip would miss her when he came home but she could not think about that.

Perhaps Matthew would consider everything she had said and move his son closer to Trembath? Even if he did not there was nothing she could do and now she could not even write to Pip. It would be best simply to disappear. Both Matthew and Pip would soon forget her. She had, after all, been here just a short time.

When she heard the taxi coming up the drive she went down and put her suitcases by the front door. She was thankful that Biddy was not in the house. She could not have faced the inquisitive little face and the interested questions.

She stood outside the door of Matthew's study and steeled herself to go in. It would be the last time that she would ever see him and she had to do this right. She knocked and went straight in before he could answer, and was a little taken aback to find that he was sitting staring into space. She had expected to see him busy and to have to face irritated eyes. Instead he got slowly to his feet and simply looked at her.

'The taxi's here,' she managed. 'I'm going now, Matthew.' He just went on looking at her and she shivered at the intent stare. 'Thank you for everything...'

'Including last night?'

'Don't! Please don't,' she choked, and she turned to the door blindly. His voice stopped her just as she was about to escape.

'Sophie?' he said deeply. 'Just one favour... Say my name in that husky voice before you go.' She thought he was taunting her and she turned to face him, tears blinding her.

'Oh, Matthew,' she reproached softly, and then she flew out of the house. Within seconds she was away, going down the drive for the last time, the sound of the sea in her ears. She didn't look back because she could not bear to see Trembath. She would never see it again—and she would never see Matthew.

She was told that the train would be late but Sophie hardly noticed. She stood on the windy platform, her luggage at her feet, and she saw nothing but Matthew's face. She could see his eyes, his black, shining hair and the strongly moulded lines of his jaw and cheeks.

She remembered how he had made love to her. How fierce it had been and then how gentle. The last sight of him lingered more than anything else, though—how he had looked when he had asked her to say his name. She had expected taunting, expected to see a sardonic look on his face, but she had not. In her tears and her panic to escape she had missed the thing that haunted her now—the stricken expression in his eyes. The feeling of wounding him came back so strongly that she knew she had to see him and find out why.

The taxi had gone, the man at the ticket booth told her.

'He's gone for his breakfast, m'dear. Back before long, though; that's his stand.' He pointed to a parking place in the station yard and she looked at him with agitated eyes.

'I have to get to Trembath House.'

'Why, he just brought you from there,' the man reminded her in surprise, and Sophie nodded, biting her lip.

'Forget something, did you?' he enquired and she looked at him desperately.

'I did. Can I leave my cases with you? I can't wait for the taxi. I'll walk.'

'It's a fair stretch,' he pointed out dubiously, but when she looked even more agitated he got out a piece of paper and drew a rough map.

'Short cut,' he told her. 'Misses out the village. It's still a good walk, though, and the taxi could have you there sooner, even after his breakfast.'

'I can't wait,' she repeated. She gave him her cases and set off, too much in a turmoil to linger even for a second. Matthew had said last night that he needed her. Perhaps he had meant it. She hurried along, going over in her mind every little thing that had happened since she had been here.

Many times there had been this feeling between them but he had always drawn back. In London he had been jealous about Andrew, possessively protective, but still he had drawn back. Only last night, having thought that she'd been lost to the sea, had he let his emotions free, and now he was feeling guilt—guilt because she was young, guilt because she was Quentin's daughter and no doubt even more guilt because she had left him.

When she finally topped the last rise and saw Trembath House below her there was such a strong feeling of homecoming that she started to run fast. The little map had guided her over the moorland and she was now approaching the house from behind. There was a gate that led from the moor and Sophie let herself into the garden at the back and opened the back door, praying that she had not made another mistake.

The door was stiff and at first she thought it was still locked but she should have known better; Matthew hardly ever locked doors and finally it gave with such a noise that she almost fell into the warmth of the kitchen, and was startled and flustered when she found that he was there. He was making himself a cup of tea and he stared at her as if he couldn't believe his eyes.

'Sophie!' he said hoarsely. 'I didn't hear the taxi come back.'

'I walked over the moor.' In fact she had run most of the way and she was out of breath, shaking with the effort. She saw him clench his hands and her eyes moved over his face. She had never seen him look like this before, so drawn and pale.

'Did you forget something?' he asked stiffly, and she nodded, never taking her eyes from his.

'I forgot you,' she said desperately. 'It was like being torn apart. I can't go away, Matthew. Even if you don't want me just let me hang around—please.' Her last word was just a whisper and his eyes darkened as he looked at her, but he didn't move.

'I'm afraid to believe what I'm hearing,' he told her quietly. 'I took a beating this morning and I can't take it again. Get your breath, Sophie, and tell me exactly what you mean.'

'I want to be with you,' she whispered, scared now that she had made a mistake. 'I don't want to be anywhere else. I can't be happy anywhere else.'

'It's the house,' he surmised heavily. 'It's the damned house. That's what pulled you back.'

'It is not the house,' she almost shouted, glaring at him in frustration. 'What do I care about the house unless you're in it? Do you think I behave with other people as I behaved with you last night? Do you think I throw myself at everybody I see? Do you think...?'

When she came to her senses she saw that he was smiling, the terrible tension gone from his face.

'Just keep going,' he begged. 'I could stand here and listen to you raging all day and night, just for the sight of you.'

She gave him a pleading look but he didn't move, and she hung her head to escape from the blaze of his eyes.

'I love you, Matthew,' she murmured huskily, and he was beside her in two strides, his arms closing round her, his hand tilting her face to his hungry mouth.

'What have you done with your luggage, my adorable little maniac?' he muttered between passionate, frustrated kisses. 'Why did you walk back?'

'I ran,' she confessed breathlessly. 'I left everything at the station and raced back because I thought I'd hurt you.'

'You did,' he told her quietly, looking down into her face. 'Last night I looked at you when you were asleep and I wanted to wake you up, to make love to you again, but you looked so young, lying there, and I felt guilty, as if I was forcing you to give up all your plans and dreams. And you're Quentin's daughter.'

'I'm Sophie Grant,' she told him fiercely. 'I'm me. I've been alone for a very long time—even when he was alive. I want to be loved. I want *you*.'

'Oh, Sophie, darling, you've got me,' he said thickly. 'You've had me since you walked through the front door on that first day.' He dropped a kiss on her soft lips and smiled into her eyes. 'In spite of my guilt and in spite of the beating you gave me I've been sitting in here wondering how soon I could come to London and find you, how I could get you to come back to me.'

'You have?' Her face lit up, and he snuggled her close to him.

'Sophie, my love, I can't keep away from you. Haven't I made that clear already? I don't think I'm ever going to be able to keep my hands off you either.'

'Please don't try,' she begged demurely, and he gave a shout of laughter as he swung her up into his arms.

'I can last out until we go back to fetch your luggage; after that we'll see.'

* * *

In the afternoon the storm came back but Sophie loved it. She was wrapped in Matthew's arms, safe and warm, his passionate desire for her leaving her tired and happy.

'I love you,' he murmured against her skin, and she drew back to look at him seriously.

'You don't have to, Matthew,' she said softly. 'I'll be content to love *you*. If one day you can get over your feelings for Delphine——'

His reaction shocked her. He rolled over and pinned her to the bed, his eyes blazing.

'Delphine?' he asked harshly. 'Why does she have to come between us? You only saw her once when you were thirteen years old!' Sophie's stunned expression finally penetrated his anger and he relaxed, moving back on to his side and curling her against him. 'Why did you mention Delphine?' he asked, with a sigh. 'I never talk about her.'

'But you think about her,' she said quietly. 'That's why I went away. I wasn't sure if I could face having the thought of another woman between us. Every time you look sad I know it's because you're missing her.'

Matthew turned her towards him, his hand tight on her chin as he tilted her face.

'You mean I was in danger of losing you because of that?' he asked in a stunned voice. 'You thought I was still in love with Delphine? Sophie, I *never* loved her! She was a cheating bitch, the hardest woman I've ever known, and finally she abandoned Philip. It may be a terrible thing to say but I was glad she could never come back.'

'I thought you still loved her. I thought you kept Pip at that school because he was so like her that he reminded you of her and it made you unhappy.'

'My God! It looks as if I'll have to tell you every thought that runs through my mind in case you have one of your attacks of working things out.' He looked down at her sternly. 'You're not very good at working things out. Don't do it!'

'You're angry,' she assessed worriedly, and he watched her enchanting face for a minute and then laughed, hugging her close to the warmth of his body.

'When we're married,' he mused, 'I'll have to give you a run-down on the state of my mind each morning, otherwise you may have altered my life before nightfall.'

'Are we getting married?' Sophie asked in a beguiling voice, and he rained heated kisses on her face before cupping it in his warm hands.

'As soon as I can get it arranged,' he stated. 'I'm not letting you out of my sight again.' He brushed her soft lips with his. 'I'm not even sure I can let you out of my arms again,' he breathed into her mouth.

When she finally lay back, flushed and happy, Matthew said more soberly, 'Perhaps I'd better tell you about Delphine. Maybe it will explain a lot of things, although you won't really want to know some of them.'

'I want to know,' she said seriously. 'You can't just go on protecting me, Matthew, and if I'm going to be your wife we have to share things.'

'All right.' He sighed deeply and then folded her in his arms, ready now to tell her about the woman who had in many ways haunted her existence since she had been at Trembath.

With her grandmother it was different. Margaret Trevelyan was like a warm glow in the house, her portrait a comfort, smiling from the wall. But Delphine had always seemed like a cold ghost, her pale blue eyes and silvery fair hair always just at the back of Sophie's mind. There had always been a feeling of distaste, as if Delphine resented her presence and any hold she had on Matthew.

'She lived in London,' he began quietly. 'At that time so did I. I don't know if you remember her very well but if you do you'll know how glamorous she was.'

'She was beautiful,' Sophie murmured, and he looked down at her, hearing the wistful tone in her voice.

'Glamorous,' he corrected her softly. 'You are beautiful, my love. You're warm, generous and loving—everything that Delphine was not. She was interested in herself and nobody else. For a time I went out with her but I was never too interested, apart from for the obvious reason,' he added caustically. 'Anyway, Quentin came home to England. We met, as we usually did, and for a brief spell Quentin was hooked by Delphine's glamour.'

'Daddy?' Sophie gasped in surprise.

'I told you it might be something you didn't want to hear,' he reminded her quietly. 'You never really knew him, darling. You never had the chance. Your mother wanted you in school—she had things to do with her life; she was an academic and damned little else. I suppose that Delphine was a change from Iris's endless notes and earnest discussions; at least she was willing in bed and, sad to say, I was glad to step back and give Quentin a free hand. At least he had one leave at home with a sparkle in his eyes.'

'I can hardly believe she left you for Daddy,' Sophie muttered. 'He was really very ordinary.'

'I think there's a backhanded compliment there somewhere.' Matthew grinned. 'I keep remembering that you said I was beautiful last night. Of course, I realise you were overwhelmed by the moment,' he finished seductively, and she blushed rose-red.

'Get on with the story,' she ordered, settling firmly in his arms.

'The story,' he said grimly. 'This is where it gets unpleasant. I was merely a member of the Press at that time, not important and not too well paid. Quentin was a professor. He had status—a status which would have grown had he lived. Your father was a very clever man and was well respected. But this story went wrong when Delphine announced that she was pregnant.'

'Pip?' Sophie said in a shocked voice, and Matthew nodded.

'Yes. She announced this to me, not Quentin. She had to work out a plan of action but she had already got well on the way with it. She said it was Quentin's child. If he didn't divorce Iris and marry her she would go to the newspapers. She mentioned very sweetly that I would know all about that. It was a deliberate piece of blackmail. In the first place I knew Quentin too well to believe it, and in the second place I also knew that she had other boyfriends. I could have killed her.'

'Did Daddy know?' Sophie asked.

'He knew finally,' Matthew said grimly. 'He was stunned. He said he had never slept with Delphine—they had just gone out together, and I certainly believed him but he could not afford any scandal. Two universities were funding his work and at any hint of that sort of thing they would have dropped him flat. Even if it was proved to be false it would have done his reputation a great deal of harm.'

'So you married her,' Sophie concluded. 'Oh, Matthew, why? It was giving your life up if you didn't love her.'

'At the time it seemed a worthwhile sacrifice, stupid though it may seem now,' he said quietly. 'Quentin had stood by me always. You've no idea how much he took from my father to shield me. I knew he wasn't happy with Iris and this would have taken away the only thing he wanted—his work. In any case, I never intended to have anything to do with Delphine. There was Trembath and I planned to bring her here and then go back to London. I worked there.'

'Is that what happened?' she wanted to know, and he sounded even more grim.

'Initially. Then I started to write and I was successful. Philip was born and I just didn't trust her with a baby. I came back here to keep an eye on things and to work, and that was a mistake. She liked success. She wanted it to be a real marriage and I didn't.

'I wanted the baby, though. He was a wonderful little chap and that was where she had a hold on me. We went right back to the beginning, to her threatening to make a statement to the paper about your father. In fact it had become even more interesting from a news point of view: MAN MARRIES WOMAN TO PROTECT STEP-BROTHER'S NAME. I told her to do her worst and we would sue her together. By that time I was doing well and had a book being filmed. I was prepared to stake everything I had to get her out of my life.'

'So what happened?' Sophie asked, and he shrugged irritably.

'A wild row happened. I learned a good deal. She told me that Philip was not Quentin's but it would be too late to save his name when the truth came out. I've never seen anyone so wickedly enjoying anything... And then she just stormed out of the house. She didn't attempt to take Philip—not that I would have let her, and thank God she didn't because that's when she had the crash, in one of the narrow lanes leading out of Port Withian. She died instantly.'

They both lay there silently, wrapped in each other's arms, and Sophie thought back over her life, trying to picture her father and mother. Now she knew why her mother had looked so cold and icy at Matthew's wedding. She had known that her husband had been seeing Delphine.

It seemed outrageous that anyone could have let Matthew make that sort of sacrifice but she knew very well from her own life that the pursuit of ancient relics had been everything to her parents—more important

than her, more important than Matthew's happiness.
They had given up the happiness of two people for things
that were dead and cold.

'I love you,' she said very loudly. 'I think you were
mad, but I love you.' It brought him out of his mel-
ancholy mood and he laughed. 'You feel it necessary to
shout?'

'I want to drum it in,' she said fiercely. 'If anybody
ever tries to hurt you again...'

He pulled her on top of him, laughing up into her
face. 'A fiery-haired avenging angel,' he concluded with
a grin. 'I feel exceptionally safe. But let me know before
you act. You'll probably have the wrong end of the stick.'

'So Pip is not your son?' she mused quietly when she
had escaped from a long time of wild kisses.

'My name is on his birth certificate,' Matthew said
seriously. 'To all intents and purposes he's mine. I love
him.'

'So why send him away to school?' she questioned
softly, and he looked at her steadily before speaking.

'This house has been in my family for generations,
Sophie. There are no portraits on the walls, but if there
were you would see a remarkable likeness between my
ancestors and me, on the male side. Whatever the bride
of a Trevelyan looks like the male line is always the
same—black-haired——'

'And golden-eyed,' Sophie finished. 'I've seen the
portraits.'

'Philip is fair,' Matthew pointed out. 'Very fair, and
it's just not possible. There was a good deal of speculation in Port Withian when he was born; memories are
long in these parts and I couldn't risk having some child
in a local school questioning him about his father. We
lived for a long time in America and there it didn't
matter, but when I had to come back he went to the

school where he is now, safely out of the way of wagging tongues.'

'He's not happy,' she reminded him solemnly, and he nodded.

'I believe you, darling, but you see the problem?'

'So let's put him in some school nearby where he can be a day-boy. He doesn't have to be in the village.'

'And if they talk?' he asked.

'Let them,' she stated firmly. 'If there's any problem he'll tell one or the other of us. Then you tell him the truth, because you'll have to one day. He doesn't need to know how awful Delphine was. Just say that you married her when she was having him because you cared about her. He loves you, Matthew, and he knows you love him. It's not going to shock him.'

'Maybe I can manage it with you here,' he mused, and Sophie hugged him tight.

'Well, I'm going to be here for always and, to be strictly truthful, I think he'll be less concerned about his beginnings than he is about a certain games master.'

'You must have been born clever,' Matthew surmised, pulling her down to him, and she smiled with smug happiness.

'Never doubt it,' she said.

Later, as they lay sleepily quiet, Matthew had a thought.

'You'll have to pay back that money to the bank if you've decided to give up university,' he reminded her.

'Bother,' she muttered. 'I never thought about that. I planned to spend it.'

'I can keep you in shampoo.' He grinned, nipping at her ear. 'Or do you want to go to university after all?' he asked more quietly.

'I'm not that easy to get rid of,' she murmured, snuggling into his arms. 'I'm perfectly happy where I am, thank you.'

'Well, that's my last problem solved. Now we can concentrate on other things,' he whispered seductively, and Sophie agreed with bewitching submission.

Sophie came out of the house and started down the steps, Pip right behind her.

'I'll see to the men, Sophie,' he said importantly. 'Dad says you race about too much. He says you should rest more.'

'Rubbish!' she declared. 'I don't race about and I do not need to rest. All the same,' she finished as he looked disappointed, 'it might be a good idea for you to see to the men.'

The men in question were from the local nursery, and at the moment they were standing waiting, two huge bushes held between them. They disappeared into the garden when Pip marched forward with a 'follow me' expression on his face, and Sophie smiled. Things were going according to plan. Pip had moved school at Easter and he was now settled happily in a day-school not too far away.

'I see your foreman is on the job.' Matthew came out and put his arms round her, pulling her back against him. 'And no more bushes, if you please. Digging those deep holes nearly killed me.'

She grinned to herself. The gardener was a touch ancient and had declared that digging holes for huge bushes was too much at his age. Matthew had done it while she supervised. The only thing he would not give ground on was Pip's name.

'I intend to retain some control of this establishment,' he had said firmly. 'Being his best friend, you'll let him get away with anything. When I call him Philip he'll remember who is the head of this family.'

He asked now, his hand possessively on the slight swell of her stomach, 'Feeling tired?'

'Not a bit,' she assured him. 'Four months pregnant is nothing at all. In any case, I intend to see this thing through. When the men have finished I'll go and cast my eye over the effect.'

He laughed quietly but the smile on Sophie's face died as Pip came running back, his expression a little anxious.

'Sophie, the men are puffing and blowing a bit,' he told her.

'Well, why don't they put the bushes down?' She looked at him in surprise and he glanced worriedly at his father.

'They're not tired. I think they're annoyed. They say the holes are in the wrong place. They say they told you to make them six feet from the hedge because these bushes will grow really big.' Matthew had gone very quiet but his hands on her tightened considerably and Pip chewed his lip. 'I think they're coming to see you,' he mentioned uneasily as the sound of voices became much louder.

'Er—take them into the kitchen for tea and scones,' Sophie suggested as she carefully extricated herself from Matthew's grasp and made off for the house with some speed. 'I'll have to think this out.'

Matthew's voice halted her flight as she was halfway to the stairs and refuge. 'Sophie!'

She stopped and turned round, eyeing him warily. 'I have to rest,' she said guiltily. 'I'm quite tired.'

He let her escape, and once in the bedroom she set her mind to working out how she was going to get out of this. For once Matthew hadn't been laughing, and it was true that she had pestered him until he had stopped writing and come to dig the holes. Who would have thought that distance from the hedge was seriously important? She was only an amateur at such things, after all.

He came in when she was looking anxiously out of the window. 'Resting?' he enquired drily as he walked towards her, and she made an attempt to wriggle out of things.

'I'm sure I didn't make all that much of a mistake,' she insisted, and he eyed her sceptically.

'Only about four feet. I must be out of my mind. I'm too soft with you.'

'What's happening?' she wanted to know, and he looked very stern.

'Biddy is filling the men with scones and Philip is asking them intelligent questions—all of which is designed to cover your tracks.'

'I'm sorry, Matthew,' she said ruefully. 'What about the holes, though?'

'Oh, *those*.' He looked down into her upturned face and he didn't seem too pleased. 'The men will fill in the mistakes and dig two further holes. It's cost me ten pounds but who would want to upset the lady of the house?'

Sophie looked uneasy and he could not keep it up any longer. He started to laugh and pulled her against him, his lips brushing over hers.

'What would I do if you were normal?' he asked softly, smiling into her eyes. 'Everything about you is a delight, my own love. Don't change. We'll all keep picking up the pieces.'

She snuggled against him, sighing happily. Matthew delighted her too, and every day her love for him grew stronger.

'You're sure you don't mind having a baby so soon?' he asked quietly, tilting her glowing face to his, and she shook her head.

'I've started as I mean to go on.' She touched his face gently. 'You're happy here now, Matthew, aren't you?'

she whispered, and he cupped her face in his hands, his eyes holding hers.

'Happier than I've been in my whole life. It wouldn't matter where we were, darling. If you're there I'm happy.' He swung her up into his arms and turned to the bed. 'Everybody seems to be well occupied right now. Let's have that rest, Sophie Trevelyan.'

She smiled and wrapped her arms round his neck. Sophie Trevelyan. It sounded wonderful and as her glance slid to the portrait of her grandmother, now hanging on the wall of their room, the eyes seemed to smile back into hers. It had all worked out at last. Trembath House had shrugged off its ghosts because once again the rooms rang with laughter. Matthew had found peace and happiness and Sophie was home.

* * * * *

Thursday's child has far to go . . .
Look out next month for Patricia Knoll's
Desperately Seeking Annie, the latest book in
our exciting series.

BRIDE'S BAY RESORT

UNLOCK THE DOOR TO GREAT ROMANCE AT BRIDE'S BAY RESORT

Join Harlequin's new across-the-lines series, set in an exclusive hotel on an island off the coast of South Carolina.

Seven of your favorite authors will bring you exciting stories about fascinating heroes and heroines discovering love at Bride's Bay Resort.

Look for these fabulous stories coming to a store near you beginning in January 1996.

Harlequin American Romance #613 in January
Matchmaking Baby by Cathy Gillen Thacker

Harlequin Presents #1794 in February
Indiscretions by Robyn Donald

Harlequin Intrigue #362 in March
Love and Lies by Dawn Stewardson

Harlequin Romance #3404 in April
Make Believe Engagement by Day Leclaire

Harlequin Temptation #588 in May
Stranger in the Night by Roseanne Williams

Harlequin Superromance #695 in June
Married to a Stranger by Connie Bennett

Harlequin Historicals #324 in July
Dulcie's Gift by Ruth Langan

Visit Bride's Bay Resort each month wherever
Harlequin books are sold.

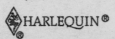

HARLEQUIN ®

BBAYG

Harlequin Romance ®

Imagine…

A picturesque town deep in the heart of the English countryside, with wide streets of old-fashioned buildings, irresistible shops and quaint tearooms.

This is

Pennington

the delightful location for an occasional series by

popular author

Catherine George.

Why not visit Pennington for yourself next month
in

#3420 Earthbound Angel

Pennington

A place where dreams come true.

Available in August wherever Harlequin books are sold.

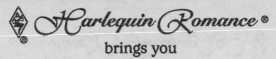

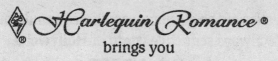

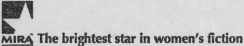